Fear Valley

When a gang of criminals commit an atrocious robbery in the bank of Harrisville, bounty hunter Jubal Thorne is quick on their trail. The murder of innocent bystanders during the robbery makes Thorne, known as Blaze, determined that the criminals will pay with their lives. The maverick leader of the group, Shannon, gives the rest of his group the slip, escaping to Fear Valley at the very end of the desert frontier. The valley is ruled by Valquez, a despot, and soon Blaze the hunter finds himself becoming the prey.

By the same author

The Broken Trail
Bandit's Gold

Fear Valley

Alex Frew

A Black Horse Western

ROBERT HALE · LONDON

Robert Hale Limited
Clerkenwell House
Clerkenwell Green
London EC1R 0HT

www.halebooks.com

Printed and bound in Great Britain by
CPI Antony Rowe, Chippenham and Eastbourne

CHAPTER 1

Harrisville was a rich little town in north-west Arizona about 200 miles from the Mexican border. The reason the town was prosperous was because of two factors. In the early days it had been a through station for the cattle drives, and was little more than a stop-off point for those who faced the problems of driving large herds across the country. They needed somewhere to house their cattle while the cowboys loaded up with food and water and let off a little steam. Then mineral wealth, gold, silver and copper had been discovered nearby. After that there was the development of the railway, which had come to the town as the great Transamerica lines went on their ceaseless march across the country after the American civil war.

This meant that from being a rough, tough, border town with one sheriff and few buildings, the town had developed into a thriving community with a white-painted clapboard school, not one but two churches, a large trading-post for those going further south, and most importantly of all, for those businessmen who traded their mineral wealth in the area, a large and flourishing bank.

The bank was well protected and that, as far as River Shannon and the Ferris gang saw it, was a problem. The gang consisted of the three Ferris brothers – Tom, Jim and Dave, hence the name, and River Shannon. They were known to all and sundry as the Ferris gang from robberies committed in Kansas and Wyoming, moving states rapidly to avoid being caught. The gang had originally consisted of the three brothers and they had picked up their fourth member when they came to Arizona to escape some of the heat their robberies had generated. The new member came from the territory, and although he didn't like them all that much they were a way of helping him get the riches he craved. Shannon, who had done some mining in this area, had been the first to suggest that they tackled Harrisville.

'That ain't no use,' said Jim, who had more capacity for abstract thought than the other two. 'That town's sewn up. They got real good defences against robbery.'

'Sure, they would have,' said Shannon. 'That's because they're rich.' The gang digested this information. They were in a saloon in Tucson and none of them had much money except that which they had gained from stick-ups over the last few weeks. Their money would soon be gone and then they would have to resort to more petty robberies or try and find work. None of them wanted to work; they had tried that and didn't like it much. This proposed robbery sounded like work too. In the past they had tackled stores, way stations, and even the odd trading post. The latter was for the simple reason that they wanted supplies and didn't have the money to buy them. A real bank, possibly with real armed guards, was not high on their agenda.

'Look,' said Shannon, 'the more petties you do, the better the chance of being caught, then you get in the hoosegow or hanged for picking up not much money. This way you get the real rewards for your effort. I'm telling you, boys, it's worth it, and all we have to do is plan real carefully.'

He had to spend another hour talking over the matter with them, spending what little money he had on drinks and painting the results of the robbery in glowing terms before they gave in to his pleas.

'It will be easy if we do it right,' he said.

So it was a week or so later that River Shannon, freshly washed and shaved, wearing a good suit, walked into the Harrisville Credit & Loan bank and cased the prospective job. He was a young man of average height, not too bad looking but he was not dressed in his travelling clothes – he had stopped off at a hotel he could not afford and changed his appearance so that he looked quietly prosperous. After doing his homework concerning the layout of the building, how well it was defended and how quickly the money could be accessed he quietly left, having falsely seen about getting a bank account. The best news as far as he could tell was that the town did not yet have a proper telegraph system, which meant they could not alert other areas quickly should a robbery occur.

He went back to the hotel, changed into his old clothing and went to the Trails saloon, where he met up with his three companions who were more concerned with playing cards, and apprised them of his findings. They might not have been all that bright, but they could see the advantage he had given them.

The same day, in the early evening, when the bank was due to close, he stationed his horse outside the building. He had already slipped a bandanna over his face before riding into the street. The Ferris brothers emerged from an alleyway on their own mounts, tied their reins loosely to the hitching rail outside the building – the animals could be made nervous by any shooting and might move away if they were free to do so. The brothers ran inside the building with their guns at the ready.

The street was busy that night with citizens going about their business, and it took one scream from a female bystander to alert everyone to what was going on. The fact that they nearly knocked her over on the way in might have alerted her to the situation. Shannon cursed that female as two riders appeared a few minutes later, their horses' hoofs thundering down the dusty street. They were clearly the local law intent on doing their duty. The fact that they had appeared so quickly told him that defending the bank was their priority.

Whatever else he might have been, Shannon was no coward. Instead of riding away to leave the brothers who were still busy finishing off inside the bank, he rode straight at the two men, holding the reins with one hand and shooting with the other. One of the men clapped a hand over his shoulder, tried to hang on with his good hand, failed to do so and tumbled to the dust. The other man was easy enough to deal with because the robber brought his own mount to an abrupt halt, turned her around in one fluid motion, aimed and shot the other man in the back. That individual hit the ground with a satisfying crunch, and then the criminal spurred his horse towards the bank.

All would have been well for him at that point because the three brothers were coming out laden with wealth, and they got on their steeds and rode away fast. This meant that all four criminals were primed to get away, but an outraged citizen, a big man in a derby hat, jerked Shannon by the leg as his mount moved off. The motion was enough to unseat him from his horse and ironically it was his turn to sprawl on the ground.

The good citizen ripped off the cloth obscuring Shannon's face. This was a mistake on the part of this person because he received a blow to the head with the butt of a gun that cracked his skull and he fell away. Shannon had trained his horse to wait for him if anything happened so, without having time to obscure his features, he scrabbled towards his mount, made a superb leap into the saddle and rode off, not caring who might be in front of him. He managed to trample another two men. In their own rout the brothers had gone even further, hurting women and children who had not got out of their way quickly enough.

In the old days when the town was packed with cowboys, a decent posse would have been gathered in minutes and the three of them would have been caught in hours. As the town was a civilized one, no-one was available immediately now that the law was down, so the gang were able to escape with relative ease. They still had to ride long distances and sleep out for a couple of nights, but that was no hardship at this time of year. Soon they were in another town near the border with Mexico. Although it was still on the territory side of the border it was called El Frontera and many of the buildings had a Spanish colonial feel.

The three brothers were delighted, they had taken a risk and it had paid off. None of them thought about their futures. They were able to relax and spend the money the way they wanted, which was all in the same way, on women, drink and gambling due to the limited nature of their thinking.

Shannon was delighted to find that they had managed to steal over $50,000. They were in their first day in the town when he used some of the money to buy new duds. He had been here before, indeed had led them here, and had some serious wooing to do. The future really was bright, except as he called on Alice Lovell to reintroduce himself, he felt a chill down his spine. It was as if a ghost had whispered in his ear.

At the same time a man was riding through the streets of Harrisville. This was Jubal Thorne, the bounty hunter. He stopped in front of the sheriff's office, dismounted and tied his horse's reins to the hitching post outside. The sheriff and his deputy had both survived the attack, although one was bound in bandages about the waist and the other around the shoulder.

They both saw a man in a long black coat that made him look taller than his actual height because although he was raw-boned, he did not carry a lot of excess weight. His hair was abundant and looked almost black but when he moved his head, deep coppery tones could be seen in his long mane. It was those locks, along with his ability to use his guns that had earned him his nickname.

'Blaze the bounty hunter,' said the sheriff wonderingly. 'I thought you were a figure in stories told around camp fires.'

'Guess I am,' said Blaze. 'Now, you got any descriptions?'

'Better than that.' The deputy raised up a poster with the words every robber dreaded at the bottom, the stark phrase, WANTED DEAD OR ALIVE. Above the words was an artist's impression of the men from what little the bank clerks had been able to see. Then there was a surprisingly good rendering of a fourth man.

'That's the Ferris gang, small time until now.' Blaze looked at it thoughtfully. 'Guess they bit off a bit more than they could chew.'

As he leaned over the newly minted poster his coppery hair had fallen over his face. Now, as he stood upright, his hair fell back on the left side, momentarily revealing the flesh-coloured patch over his left eye, and the scars that furrowed his forehead and neck. He stared at them with his good right eye, which they now saw was a deep, dark brown, the eyelashes almost as long as that of a woman, as he restored the hair on the left so it concealed his damaged features. He must once have been a very handsome man. He lit a cigarillo which he stuck between his lips as he memorized the one clear face on the poster. He blew out a plume of smoke as he stepped away from the two men.

'Lucky I was around. You got the right man for the job.'

He left them and mounted his horse, the sides of his long black coat trailing down as he went to get supplies, his wide-brimmed Stetson throwing his face into shadow. People shied away from him as he progressed along the street towards the sun that hung low in the sky like a blood-red eyeball. He had a long ride ahead of him and he was going to start tonight.

Outside of the lawman's office, the deputy started to hang up the poster but the sheriff stayed his hand.

'I wouldn't bother. They're all coming back, one way or another.'

CHAPTER TWO

Jubal Thorne did not take long to find, and then get on the trail of the gang. The town had offered to send a posse with him but he had declined for a number of practical reasons. The men who would make up such a body would, by definition, be amateurs at this kind of tracking. They would set off in fine spirits only to find as the long and weary hours went on that they were in a dogged pursuit, not a short chase. Out of a party of, say, six, perhaps four would give up and ride home. The other two would stick to their guns for a few more miles, and then they too would argue that that the robbers had been lost, only to depart soon after.

Thorne knew that only logic could prevail out here in the wilderness where the purple sage seemed to stretch for an endless distance until the country gave way to a rugged landscape of deep canyons and high mesas. He also knew that the robbers wanted an easy time; they would head for the nearest town where they could blow their ill-gotten gains.

That is why he rode into the streets of El Frontera less than two days later, just as the dusk was beginning to fall and the sun was once more a fiery red ball in the sky. His horse plodded wearily into the wide, long main street. He did not have many feelings for the beast either way, but he found a livery where he tossed a few silver dollars to the white-haired keeper to feed and water the animal. The rest would do them both good. He was saddle sore from his long journey and his shoulders ached.

As he looked around the stables, his expert eye took in the big greys and quarter-horses housed there. The horses were another clue that he was on the right track, but he didn't say anything to the keeper of the livery. He did not as yet know the name of the youngest robber, and knew that this inquiry would mark him out. He had a feeling the livery keeper might have been bribed by that person to let them know when a new hombre came into town asking a few awkward questions. Thorne walked down the street in the gathering dusk, the sun now low on the horizon like half a blood orange. The few buildings he passed were of no interest to him, a general store, a barber shop; a place that offered hot baths (although he made a note to check in, and use their services once he had stocked up his belly with some vittles); and an eatery called Ma's.

He finally came to a spur-jangling halt in front of an adobe-and-brick building marked above the somewhat weathered door with the equally weathered sign 'Sheriff's Office'.

To his left, high on a hill was a large, well-lit house wrought in a plain style, but with long sash windows and

14

a double-wide oak front door. He wondered idly who the house belonged to before turning his attention to the office. He lit one of his thin black cigarillos and sat down in the old willow chair outside the building, enjoying his first real rest in two days.

'Penny for them,' grunted a shadowy figure at his side. He turned his head, twin plumes of smoke exhaling from his nostrils. Two men stood there. One was obviously in late middle age, and the other a gangly, shock-haired youth who appeared to be barely out of his teens.

'Just contemplating a visit to the sheriff,' said Thorne.

'Then you're in luck. I guess you can come in. We've got most of the home comforts, even a spare bed if you need it.'

'I'll pass on that for the moment, but I'll come in with you.'

The sheriff unlocked the door and the three of them went inside. The office was functional, with a gun-rack against the side wall, a large desk at front, several wooden chairs, bare floorboards. The cells at the bottom of the office were unoccupied, all three of them. The iron-bellied stove in the corner was churning out heat. The sheriff put on a pot of coffee and shared it with the other two in pewter mugs. He produced some cold beef and bread, presented on a tin plate, which the visitor consumed gratefully.

'Dan Clayton,' he said, 'this here miscreant is Mikey. Now who have we here?'

'Jubal,' said the new arrival, gratefully drinking down the tarry black substance. His hair drew back a little as he drank and the young deputy stared in fascination at what little was revealed of the scars and the flesh-coloured patch.

'Reckon you have to tell us a little more,' said the sheriff, seating himself comfortably behind the desk and putting his feet up. 'Like why Blaze has decided to visit our little back water.'

'You reason well,' said Blaze. Now that his identity had been revealed he saw little point in holding back. 'I'm here for a little information.'

'Sure. If I think it's the right thing to do, I'll tell you,' said Clayton. He had a direct, challenging look that did not flinch away from the baleful appearance of the new arrival.

'I'm looking for these men.' Blaze unfolded the copy of the wanted poster and threw it on the desk. 'Any idea where they might be?'

'Could be around here,' acknowledged the sheriff.

'Rode in just the other day,' said Mikey. 'They got lots of money to spend.'

'Sure they have.' Clayton gave his assistant a warning look. 'How much they get away with?'

'A lot.'

'And you get the reward?'

'Happy to share it if you help me out.'

'Well, there's a low-down joint called The Lone Star owned by some Texan. You could try over there, for three of them, is all I'm saying,' said Clayton.

'And the fourth?'

'Guess that young man has ideas above his station. Get the feeling he knows this place. He got himself some fancy duds an' went up the hill to woo Alice Lovell.'

'Who is she?'

'Only the heiress to the Lovell mining corporation.

They provide most of the work around here, one way or the other.'

'That right?' Blaze took out his pistols, checked them over and put them back into the pockets of his long coat.

'Them's fancy irons,' said Mikey, a note of admiration in his voice.

'Tools of the trade, the old doglegs are too big for real action,' said Blaze. 'These are short-barrelled Peacemakers. Ain't too accurate on the long shot, but then again I get real close to ones I want to shoot.' He lifted his jacket to reveal a soft leather holster under his left armpit. 'Keep a snub-nosed revolver in here in case any of these beauties jam. It's kinda saved my life before.' Mikey was now agog with hero-worship.

'We don't want trouble around here,' said Clayton.

'Tell you what,' said the bounty hunter. 'You wait outside the saloon and if anything kicks off that shouldn't you haul in there and sort it out. Get Mikey here to watch out for that suitor up on the hill and give us a twin salute with his guns to let me know the guy's ready. You up for it, Mikey?'

'Sure am, mister.'

'Wait a minute.' Clayton looked a little dizzy, as well he might at this sudden onslaught of ideas. 'You're walking in here and taking over, Blaze? I guess what they told me about you wasn't true.'

'What?'

'That you was a gentleman.'

'Sure, I can be real gentle when I need to be,' said Blaze, 'but right now you've got four miscreants here in your town, one of whom is making it plain that he's after the daughter of a rich man. Don't think anyone really wants that kind around here, do you?'

'I guess you got me there,' admitted the sheriff.

'So you'll let me get on with the job?' Blaze looked at the sheriff with his one good eye. For some reason the sheriff could not look away, he could hardly blink.

'I suppose it makes sense. We sure can't let them do just what they want around here. Who's to say what they're going to do next? Besides, you won't have much trouble with the three brothers; they've been living it up in the hotel part of the saloon since they got here. The local whores are real grateful. Mikey?'

'Yes, sir?' asked that young person.

'Do as the man asks, keep an eye on the Lovell property and if you see Shannon so much as put a whisker around the door, you alert me. OK?'

'No bother, but say, can I shoot him down?' asked the deputy plaintively. 'I'm getting better all the time.'

'You blamed fool, you'll get your head shot off,' said Clayton. 'Just get out there and do as you're told.' The young man gave a wide grin at this, snapped his wide-brimmed hat on his head and disappeared. He was at that time of life, an age when everything seems good and death is a distant prospect.

'He's a good lad,' said Clayton, 'my cousin's eldest boy. Thing is, he's got a feeling about Alice. She's a real beautiful girl, you should see her, got a figure that'd rouse a granite statue to whistle. The thing was, until this Shannon came along, she was kind of encouraging his interest.'

'Shannon?'

'Yep, River Shannon, that's the name of her current suitor. Knew her before when he was a young miner, now he's back as if he's some kind of returning hero.'

'That's all right,' said Blaze, 'he'll be going on the back of a buckboard with the rest.' He picked up his dark hat, which was still dusty with the yellow alkali soil of the semi-desert beyond the town, and the two men moved out of the office together.

Shannon was blessing his good fortune that he was finally with the woman he loved. This was a word that he would barely have dared to think in the old days when he had first seen her in the town. He was only a couple of years older than the girl, they had first met when they were children. Even now he was just twenty-three years old.

He had come back that first night after the robbery to call on her, with flowers in his hand and his good suit on, barely daring to breathe. But she had been more than gracious, asking him to come and see her again.

When it came to her part, she recognized that he seemed manlier than she remembered. He had done well for himself too, just in the same way as her father, who had taken a few mining opportunities, had ended up creating the Lovell corporation. River told her that he had opened up a clothing business in Tucson, that he was making good money. Above all else he told her that he loved her. There was no impropriety in their meeting. Even in a remote town like this relations between the sexes until they were officially engaged had to be observed by a chaperone. Since her father was away on some business at his mines, and her mother had died in childbirth, this fell to Miss Ella, a large, elderly black woman who had been with the family since before the girl was born. When they were together, she sat with them and looked at Shannon in a way that dared him to do so much as try to hold hands with the girl. This did not stop him passing a few whispered messages to her at the doorway at the end of the night. Nor would it interfere with his newest plan.

On the second night of their meeting, Shannon had already acquired a sturdy little wagon and a hardy pair of mustangs. The wagon was loaded with a few supplies. He had already acquired the rest of the money, which he had hidden in a convenient space inside the wagon where no casual agent would possibly find it. He had contrived to get most of the money because after spending a few hundred in the saloon, the brothers had not needed a penny. The gleeful owner of the saloon was letting them build up a huge bill for obvious reasons.

Alice, not knowing of his connection with the others, had already agreed to his whispered proposal. Tonight he intended to take her at her word. Whether it took silencing Ella or sneaking her out after they had officially parted, he was taking Alice away with him and getting married to the richest girl in the district.

The sheriff stood with Blaze and looked up at the saloon along with the gunman. This had once been a fairly ornate building created about the time of the Gadsden Purchase when those who created the town had fairly high hopes. In front of the building was a square porch jutting out from the rest of the plank walk. Up above, there was a walkway that went outside all of the rooms, protected by a white wooden rail. Lights were on in three of the rooms. Blaze assessed the situation with his one expert eye then turned to the sheriff.

'Keep a look out on things from out here, Clayton, if you don't mind.'

'You won't cause a riot?' asked the sheriff. 'That place has some mean customers.'

'I'm meaner,' said Blaze, leaving the man behind.

His boots clumped on the wooden surface of the plank walk, making his spurs jingle musically with each step. He drew in a deep breath, opened the batwing doors and stepped inside. Directly in front of him was a long bar, evidently well-stocked with whatever the miners and cowboys around this part needed. They wanted chiefly rotgut whiskey, mescal, tequila and dark beer, judging by the contents of the shelves behind the counter and the tapped barrels lying to one side. Just for a second he was almost overwhelmed by a longing to go over to the counter, order two bottles of whiskey and retreat into the bottle. But he had already been down that route a long time ago and it didn't work for him or anybody really. The barman, wearing an apron that might once have been white, took one look at the newcomer and turned his head away, pretending to polish a glass.

The tables were crowded with groups of men drinking, smoking and swearing incessantly and playing cards, probably faro and poker. One or two had not exactly fair maidens sitting on their laps. At one time he would have condemned such things, now he took them in with a dispassionate glance.

To the other side, the only item of glamour was the curving staircase that led to the upper regions, the hotel part of The Lone Star. The banisters and balustrades had been made out of dark, polished oak, while the stairs were wide and opulently carpeted. Beside this curving stairway, at which stood another lady who might have been attractive if it had not been for her blackened teeth, were the traditional piano, and a grandfather clock that had long ago ceased to tell the time. The piano sat forlornly without a player which hardly mattered since the noise in the saloon was so loud a player would have been drowned out anyway.

This all stopped as the varied clientele noticed the new arrival. There was a silence that hung in the air, as substantial as the blue fog that rose above them from their cigarettes and cigars. Blaze pulled back his hair and lifted his eye patch. The only sound that could be heard was the jingling of his spurs as he marched towards the stairs.

CHAPTER THREE

The silence was broken by a scream from the not-so-young lady who had been looking on the new arrival as a potential client. What she saw coming towards her was a face that looked perfectly normal on the right side, could have been anything from thirty-five to forty-five years old. On the other side she was faced with a nightmare, a pattern of scarred lines that ran from forehead to neck as if the flesh had run like a river then solidified. But that was not what had made her scream. He had lifted the flesh-coloured eye patch, revealing that the cause of the scars had also taken away the surrounding parts of his eye yet had somehow spared the eye itself. What she saw was a glaring orb surrounded by a skeletal eye socket as if half his skull was fighting to emerge from his head. Her scream was abruptly cut off as he came even closer because her throat seemed to have closed up and she was now too terrified to scream. She crouched down, a wordless gurgle coming from somewhere inside. He ignored her, did not even notice she was there anymore and passed her almost soundlessly on the stairs, even the noise of his spurs muted by the deep carpeting.

Blaze did not wait, but kicked open the first door he came to. The first kill was almost too easy. Tom Ferris was spread across an iron framed bed on his front, still wearing his trousers, the bottle of whiskey lying on the floor a testament to this evening's work. Beside him, a half-naked woman was playing with her hair, obviously deeply unsatisfied with whatever had transpired between them. She too gave a whimper of fear as she saw the man who came into the room.

'Wake up,' said Blaze.

Tom Ferris looked up groggily, saw the twin Peacemakers pointed at him and jumped out of bed, reaching for the Colt he had used for the robbery at the same time. Blaze shot him in the heart. One shot, that was all, glad that he had allowed the man at least the chance to reach the gun. The half-naked woman ran past the bounty hunter and down the stairs without even trying to cover herself. The body in the first room was still pumping blood on the rug even as he kicked in the second door.

He did not hesitate when it came to the next robber because he was well aware that time in this case was of the essence. With barely a pause between shooting the last man, he kicked in the door of the adjoining room. Wisely, he stepped back and to one side in a fluid motion as soon as he had done so. The second brother, Jim, alerted by what had happened next door, had obviously decided to come out fighting. Blaze, if he had the time to reflect on this, would have given an inward chuckle at the thought. There was no way a robber who was quite happy to shoot an unarmed bank clerk in the face, or trample a woman and child into the soil with his horse's hoofs, would be a match for an expert bounty hunter. Just the same, he was glad he had hung back because as the door yawed wide, a fusillade of shots passed over the area in which he would have been standing if he had been stupid enough to wait.

Ducking down, Blaze threw himself into the room, making a smaller target for the would-be gunman. The skeletal-eyed bounty hunter had also guessed that none of the Ferris brothers would have reloaded their weapons since the robbery because they thought that they had got away with their vile act. This proved to be the case. Jim Ferris was standing wide-eyed against a mirrored dresser, a six-gun in each hand. The bullets all spent, a hollow clicking noise all that could be heard as he frantically tried each trigger in turn. The room was compact to say the least. The walls had once been painted cream above and green below but were now yellow from the smoke of thousands of cigarettes and cigars. More empty bottles lay on the floor beside the bed that had once contained tequila and raisin brandy. A girl who looked about fourteen was crouched naked in the opposite corner beside a washstand. Blaze did not turn his baleful gaze full on her but instead swivelled his head enough to make it plain he was speaking to her.

'You there, get out. NOW.' The girl got to her feet and scuttled out of the doorway. Although he had not turned his head fully towards her, his attention had been distracted long enough for Jim to make one last attempt at attacking his tormentor. He threw his useless weapons at the head of his would-be captor. Blaze dodged to either side as the guns flew at him, and they thudded uselessly to the ground. Only then did the second Ferris brother try to reason with him.

'Let me go, I didn't do that much, I swear.'

'You all did,' said Blaze tonelessly. 'Killing and injuring innocents without a single thought in your head and dollar signs in your eyes.' Not being one for dramatics he fired a single bullet. It took Jim in the forehead just a second later. There was the sound of breaking glass as his flailing body fell backwards and shattered the mirror behind him. He jerked a few times then sprawled limply on the dresser.

Luckily the bullet had left most of his features intact. Blaze inwardly cursed himself for shooting the man in the head. He needed someone to be able to identify the robber. It was how he made his living. Luckily he had got away with it this time.

Now he turned to the last room. An interesting line-up if you looked at it in a particular way, three dumb brothers in three rooms, all drinking and fornicating their brains out.

As far as Blaze was concerned they were all better off the surface of the earth.

He performed the same trick as before, kicking in the door and stepping back but no shots followed. Even then his suspicions were not allayed; at least one of the brothers had to have some vestiges of intelligence.

He felt a rush of cold air from the doorway that aroused his suspicions of what was going on in the room. He went in, guns at the ready only to find two thinly-dressed whores, staring wordlessly at the long window that led onto the upper walkway of the building.

They turned as he entered, and as his face became visible in the lamplight they cowered together. They were unafraid of the guns, for they had seen plenty of those in their time, but reacted with superstitious dread to the staring eye and skeletal socket facing them. It was only when he approached them as silent as a ghost, dark clothes flapping on his raw-boned frame that they moved. They shrieked in unison and fled to either side of him and out of his way. He could hear them gibbering to each other as they headed out to the corridor and down the stairs. Blaze heeded them no more as he trod out to the walkway where the lights from the rooms faintly illuminated most of the area. There was a pool of darkness down at the far end where a man might have remained concealed, crouching down as he waited for action.

Blaze, though, didn't think the remaining Ferris was the kind who would fight it out like a man. His notion bore fruit when he noticed a twin line of digits clinging to the edge of the wood just a couple of feet further on. Without a second's hesitation he stamped down with the thick leather heels of his boots. There was a howl of pain and outrage that might have been comical in different circumstances, followed by the sound of a heavy body thudding to the soft ground at the side of the hotel.

Luckily for the falling man the plank walk did not extend to that area. The gunman strained both his eyes in the direction of the sound, and was rewarded by seeing a shadowy figure rise to his feet, trying to make it away from the area. The bounty hunter did not like to lose a target.

He aimed steadily and then fired his weapon, cursing as his first shot zinged to the ground beside the man, just missing him. More to the point, as Blaze aimed again at his target, the last Ferris turned and took a potshot at his assailant. They fired at the same time, and Blaze saw the man go down, but it was the last thing he was conscious of seeing without pain and distortion for a long time. Luckily for Blaze the bullet that was aimed at him missed, but unluckily it ricocheted off one of the metal hinges holding the window open and hit him in the lower right side. The pain made him stumble forward in an involuntary manner, which would have been fine if he had been on the level. But the flimsy wooden rail, which was more of a decoration than a serious barrier gave way with a dry crack! And he found that he was pitching headlong into empty space. He was aware of thumping into the dry soil a few seconds later as the pain flooded through his body. His only hope was that he had not broken his back.

A figure came running over; it was Sheriff Clayton who looked down at him with concern written all over his face.

'Don't move, I'll get help.'

'Did I get him?' asked Blaze, his voice barely a whisper.

'Yes,' said the sheriff.

'Good,' said Blaze before passing out.

In the meantime things had not gone so well for Alice Lovell. She was with the man she thought she loved when they had heard the first gunshots.

'I thought Sheriff Clayton had started dealing with that kind,' she said, a frown marking her pretty forehead as she peered through the thick curtains at the saloon where the noise was coming from.

'Now you come away from there, Miss Alice,' demanded Ella. 'Don't you bother with such things.'

'I think she should bother,' said Shannon. He looked directly at the girl. 'Alice, I need to talk to you for a minute.'

'Miss Alice,' began the old servant.

'Ella, leave us alone for five minutes, we're adults, and I promise you there will be no impropriety.'

The servant grumbled to herself, but she could not ignore a direct order from the daughter of the manor. She bustled out of the door, glaring at Shannon as she did so.

'There is a man after me,' said Shannon. 'He is a criminal who wants revenge on me after what I did in the city.'

'What did you do?'

'I would rather not talk about it.' Like the liar he was, he knew not to reveal his story straight away.

'Come on.' The girl was impatient to know.

'It's in the past.'

'I will hit you, River, seriously, I mean it.'

'I caught him robbing a bank, threw him to the ground. There was a reward. He got years in prison, but I learned he had escaped. A mean-looking man who stops at nothing. I think he's tracked me down.'

'No! What are you going to do?'

'I'm going to get out of here. Now. But I will always think of you.'

'Take me with you!'

'I can't, you will be putting yourself in danger, and I think he has people watching us right now.'

'I don't care, you promised to marry me some time in the future. Let's get out of this place, there's a village called Hixby near here, we'll go and get married.'

'I can't subject you to that kind of danger; your father will kill me.'

'He won't, I won't let him.' The girl was thrilled by the danger, all her life she had been cosseted and sheltered by her father as far as possible from the dangers around them. At times she felt like a prisoner. Now she was with a man who would offer her some excitement and danger. Also, he was well off and good-looking. All of these factors combined to make her want his company. The girl went to see Ella and sent her off to the cellar supposedly for some wine. While the old servant was away she fetched her warmest coat and put her fur lined boots on, because she knew how cold it could get at night. She ran out of the building to the yard where he had left the wagon and they rode off. She had left a note for her father on the table in the hallway telling him about their trip to Hixby, knowing he wasn't due back until the next day.

Mikey, seeing the wagon riding down the hill, grabbed out his one gun, an old Navy Colt pistol, which could fire six shots and pointed it at the rumbling vehicle with the couple at the helm.

'Halt,' he shouted, 'or I'll shoot.' But the wagon did not halt and it struck him that his life was in danger as it bore down on him at a fast speed imparted by the hoofs of the two hardy mustangs and the steepness of the hill. He jumped to one side and his body impacted with the ground, jarring his shoulder. On the wagon, the girl gave

Shannon a light punch.

'Why did you do that to him?'

'He was always gonna get out of the way,' said Shannon lightly.

'OK, but he was just concerned for me. I like Mikey.' The girl leaned lightly against Shannon as they moved swiftly off into the darkness. There was a solidity about him that thrilled her.

She was experiencing real adventure.

Blaze woke up. He was in a comfortable bed. His eye patch had been replaced. The bed was in a room that could only have belonged to a man, no feminine traces at all. There was a clock on the opposite wall and a shotgun in the corner. Clayton sat by his side on an old wooden chair, leaning over as he saw the bounty hunter regain consciousness. Blaze felt a tightness at his side and wriggled a little to ease it off. He had been bandaged but the wound still hurt like hell.

'What happened?' The words came out in a croak as if his throat had been lined with sandpaper.

'You lost a helluva lot of blood. I got you back here, helped by some of the local boys and the doc took out the bullet and bandaged you up. Heck of a thing. He said if it had hit you direct you'd have been torn in two.'

'I've had worse.'

'Doc took a glance at that eye while he was in and you was out,' said Clayton. 'Said he'd seen nuthin' like it except once when he was helping identify the corpses from a real bad fire.'

'Uh-huh.' The bounty hunter made a non-committal

noise at this.

'Like to talk about what happened? He said the melting flesh must've made some kind of cowl and that's what saved your eye on that side. Reckons the dead flesh would've dried up and sloughed off in a few weeks.' Blaze did not so much as turn his head at this, but he touched his eye patch to make sure it was adjusted properly, then pulled his hair into place. He got to his feet and winced at the pain.

'Whoa! What do you think you're doing?'

'Getting ready to ride, that's what. Now give me a hand with these duds.'

Reluctantly Clayton assisted the gunslinger. Once dressed, Blaze immediately seemed to feel better. He soon realized that the sheriff's home abutted onto the jail. The sheriff followed him as he made his way out of the wood-and-adobe building and into the main street. It was now daylight, not much after dawn. Looking further up and across the wide road he saw a flat cart, on which Mikey was using his powerful arms to lift on the last of three burlap-wrapped forms. The deputy lifted across a tarpaulin to keep them out of direct sunlight.

'Well, Sheriff, that sure was mighty good of you,' said Blaze. 'What's the arrangement?'

'Easy enough. You take those three sons-of-bitches back to Harrisville so we can claim some sort of reward.'

Blaze heard the 'we' in the sentence but gave the man his due. Clayton had already done more than enough to earn his share.

'One more to track down,' said Blaze. 'Unless you got the money too?' He glared at Clayton with one eye that could see into a man's soul. Clayton looked back at him in an equally direct manner.

'There wasn't a penny in any of the rooms. Those bums were relying on their friend to look after their stake and pay their bills. Pretty smart of them for a bunch of dumb oxen.'

'So where's the money then?'

'Well, see, you were up so quick, like a racehorse and I didn't have time to tell you the other news.'

'Hey, you!' cried a voice laced with raw emotion. A big man with grey hair, a prominent nose and jaw, and a usually generous mouth that was now a thin line, advanced towards them. In his right paw he held an ivory sheet of notepaper with a pattern of intertwined primroses at the top. From his well-cut clothes and general bearing, Blaze took him to be the father of Alice Lovell.

'What's the meaning of this?' he asked, waving the piece of paper around as if it was a proclamation. 'Who's that benighted bastard who's made off with my daughter to marry her in Hixby?'

'I think his name might be Shannon,' said Blaze evenly. 'Believe he's a local boy?'

'River Shannon?' said the big man. 'Son of a miner, a miner himself come to think of it. Went a while back, heard some rumours he did well in business.'

'If that business was robbery he did well to the tune of $50,000 in Harrisville,' said Blaze. 'See those lumps of carrion over there? He was their leader.'

'Got back from checking out some new workings early this morning,' said Martin Lovell. 'Marty Lovell.'

'They call me Blaze.'

'You look like you know what you're up to,' admitted the old man grudgingly.

'I'll saddle up right away, and after getting supplies I'll get on their trail. They'll have stopped somewhere in the night, so I'll be able to catch up with them.'

'You do that; you'll get a good reward.' Lovell looked down bitterly. Blaze had noticed something about the man's gait, now he realized that Lovell was clutching an ebony walking stick with an ivory handle. 'Crooked this leg in the mines when I was starting out,' he said bitterly, 'or I'd ride after the bastard myself.'

'Seems like we both got the same idea in mind,' said Blaze. 'Sorry to meet you in these circumstances, Mr Lovell.' He began to move towards the trading post.

'Wait a minute, this Shannon, is he really dangerous?' asked Lovell.

'He killed a man, fractured the skull of another and trampled down women on his way out of town after the robbery,' said Clayton.

Inwardly, Blaze cursed the man for saying these words. A simple 'yes' would have been more than ample for purpose.

'Then, Sheriff, you've got to help Blaze out.'

'I don't need any help.'

'I trust you, I don't know why, because we just met, but as far as I can see you've got one eye and that's my girl out there. I want the best chance there is of getting her back. Sheriff, you've got to help him get her, the two of you will have the best chance.'

'Sure, Mr Lovell, I can do that.' Clayton looked squarely

at Blaze. 'Mr Lovell here, he brought a lot of peace and prosperity to this town over the last twenty years. Used to be the kind of place you would have a fifty-fifty chance of surviving if you had a disagreement on a Saturday night. His mines and my law have made the place livable. I'd do this for him as a private citizen. Besides which, the daughter of a prominent citizen has been kidnapped, that makes it my business. I'm willin' to go.'

Blaze glared at Clayton, but he knew when he was defeated. Besides, if things got bad and he needed to work on his own he could always arrange for Clayton to be 'accidentally' knocked out while the business was conducted. Another pair of eyes might be useful too.

'All right,' he said, 'but be aware I can't guarantee anybody's safety. I'll just get everything prepared. You can get that deputy of yours to give me a hand, but you can break the bad news to him that he's going to be sheriff for the immediate future.'

'He's a good boy,' said Clayton. 'Do you know that last night he was nearly killed trying to stop Shannon's wagon and pair? Nearly got trampled, yet he's still out here first thing bagging up them Ferris turds.'

'I thought my daughter liked Mikey,' said Lovell. 'I would have encouraged the match too. Then she would have stayed in town, and that's the most important thing to me.' His eyes were like twin agates as he looked at the two men. 'Bring her back, bring back my baby. She's the most precious thing in the world to me.'

CHAPTER FOUR

The girl was full of excitement as the wagon rolled off into the darkness. They travelled for a couple of hours along a well-defined track at a good speed. It was getting so cold Shannon deemed it no longer safe to travel any further, pulling off the road to a sheltered spot that he seemed to know of. There they made camp amidst a clump of trees and bushes. The girl was full of talk, wanting to share the experience with him. For a while the ex-miner seemed to keep up the pretence, then he got her to get some shut-eye so they could both be fresh the next day.

Rather disappointingly he was the perfect gentleman with her, allowing her to sleep in the wagon amid his fairly extensive supplies. If Alice had been thinking clearly she might have wondered why he needed so much if they were just going to the next small town to get married. Instead she lay awake and thought about her impending wedding to a man she barely knew. Of course, she could have a white wedding at a later date, but she knew this wasn't just about her forthcoming nuptials. Her act of defiance also had something to do with her father and the way he tried to control her actions every minute of the day. Well, this might not be the first of her acts of rebellion, but it would certainly be her last. As for River Shannon, he seemed quite mild in general, a man she would soon be able to bend to her will. With that final thought she drifted off to sleep.

Sleep was not to last for that long. She felt the blankets being pulled off her and she heard his urgent voice.

'Time to get going.'

To her befuddled eyes it looked as if it was still dark outside, but she got up and did what she had to do before riding up front with him. The dawn was barely breaking as they headed out onto the road.

'Can't be long until we're in Hixby,' she said, clutching his arm tightly, feeling the muscles under his fringed green jacket.

'Yep,' he said briefly, but as they rode on doubts began to percolate through her mind.

'Wait a minute, you're going off the road, and this looks as if we're heading for the wilds.' Indeed her surmise was correct; she now realized they were speeding over low green terrain that no carriage had travelled for many years, if ever.

'It's all right,' he told her, 'just taking a longer route to fool them who's sure to chase us. Tell you what, get into the back and relax and I'll shout to you when we're there.'

Once more she did not see any reason to doubt him, surely this heading off into a region of stony bluffs and low plant life was for the reason he was giving?

The interior was much more inviting than being up

front where it was cold in the dawn. Once in the back of the vehicle she rested on the blankets he had given her the night before. It was only then, as she looked around, that it struck her that they seemed to have a lot of supplies for a short journey. Although she was headstrong Alice was not a stupid girl, and her suspicions were to be confirmed by an unexpected event. As the wheels rattled across one particularly rough stretch of terrain, one of the floorboards popped up.

Intrigued by this, she investigated the loose plank since she had nothing better to do with her time. At the very least she could put it back into place. She saw at once from the slightly splintered edge that the board and the one beside it had been levered up quite recently. Instead of putting it back in place as had been her first intention, she lifted the second board, only to find in the space below a cloth bag stuffed full of paper. Since she was only human she pulled this out and studied its contents for a full five minutes before she put it back and replaced the boards. It was not in her nature to try and make excuses. She did what she had to do. She struggled her way to the front of the coach and sat down beside River.

'We're not going to Hixby to get married, are we?' Her voice framed the question more like a statement. The one thing about the robber was that he caught on quickly. He gave her a sideways glance as he continued to spur the horses onwards.

'You sure are good at catching on. No, we're going to a sheltered spot until the posse – because they're sure to send one – gets off our trail. I know a place where we'll be safe for a while.'

'Is that so?' The girl produced a gun she had also found in the supplies at the back. 'River, I've made the biggest mistake of my life, but that doesn't mean I have to continue to be a fool. Take me home.' But even as she was speaking he was slowing down the horses and now they came to a panting halt.

'What're you going to do? Hold that thing to my head for the whole journey back?'

'If I have to.'

'Then you're making a mistake.' As he spoke he shoved the hand holding the pistol upwards and unceremoniously pushed her off the seat. She had never really handled a gun in her life before and the action sent the weapon spinning out of her hand while the fall to the ground jarred the breath out of her body.

The landing had distressed her more than hurting her. With a muffled curse he jumped down beside her with a contrite look on his handsome features.

'I'm sorry I had to do that. I thought you were going to blow my head off.' She got up and faced him. Her skirts were stained with the yellow alkali dust that covered every-thing around here.

'I was going to blow your head off if you didn't take me home.'

'You changed your mind quickly! What in the name of the big man in heaven is wrong with you?'

'I saw it all; I saw what was beneath those planks on the bed of the wagon. You've been stealing money. Lots of money.'

'Listen, I wasn't lying to you, my love. I really do love you, I thought you were putting me in danger. I can explain about the money.'

'What?'

'Those renegades who came to town were thieves, robbers, they were a gang. I only fell in with them and learned about their terrible trade by accident.'

'What renegades?'

'Come on, I'm sure Ella must have said something about them, that woman knows everything that's going on.'

'She did mention some undesirables had lodged at the saloon hotel, and that you came to town at the same time. Seeing that money I put two and two together.'

'Well, you made five. I took the money all right, but it was only because I knew where it was from listening in on them when they thought I couldn't hear them. When you said you were going to go away with me that drove everything from my head, it happened so fast.'

'But you didn't even head for town.'

'I told you, they'll try and stop us. We'll hide for a few days then we'll go and get married as we planned, and we'll take the money back with us and hand it over to the authorities.'

For a moment it could have gone either way. The girl could have disbelieved him and fought to the end out here in this wildness of eye-catching purple and green. They were now riding down into some kind of stony gorge she now noticed, having been in the back of the wagon for some time.

Or she could go along with him.

'But where are you going? At least let me know that much.'

'I was going to let you know when we got there, it's called Hidden Valley, and you're in for a pleasant surprise. No-one will find us there. I'm sorry I struck you but I thought my life was in danger.' He held out his hand. 'Let me help you back up.'

For a moment the girl held back, and then her pretty face lit up in a smile as she took his hand. As he pulled her closer she swung with the palm of her left hand and caught him a stinging blow on the face.

'What the hell was that for?'

'For pushing me off like that. Now help me up, we have a trip to take.'

He rubbed the reddened flesh as he helped her back on to the padded seat at the helm of the wagon but carefully concealed his smile of satisfaction as he got up beside her and they rode off towards their destiny.

Blaze looked at the trail with an experienced eye.

'This is where they brought the wagon,' he said. 'I can see the fresh marks made by iron horseshoes.'

'Yep, that's surely true,' said Clayton. 'Don't look as though they're heading for Hixby, though.'

'Did you really expect them to be going that way?'

'Nope.'

'Then let's find out where they really went.'

The pair had been riding along steadily since early light just after their encounter with the girl's father. Neither of them were great speakers by nature and they rode along side by side in silent agreement, only stopping now and then to confirm their destination. At times Clayton lost the track but then Blaze – even with his eye patch on – would point out where they had to go.

He did not think much about the Ferris brothers, except to experience a slight degree of satisfaction. He had managed to find a local mortician who had agreed to take the bodies back to Harrisville and get them there in a reasonable condition, and for quite a fair price considering the time and trouble it would take to do this. His satisfaction was tempered by the thought of all the trouble it would take to get the final member of the gang.

As they moved along, tracking down the wagon, the terrain began to change to a remarkable degree. The purple sage began to give way to more stony ground, yet still with clumps of green here and there and the odd cacti, but nothing like the ones found in the desert further to the south. The ground began to slope downwards to a remarkable degree to the point where Clayton was moved to express his concern.

'Are you sure we're on the right track? Why the hell would he have brought her here?'

'See, Clayton, I ain't a local boy. Maybe you can think of a reason.'

'I can think of something,' said Clayton at last, 'but you might think it's a bit unlikely.'

'We've gone much faster than any wagon with these here mounts, if we keep going for a reason we'll get them.'

'Well, I've heard rumours that there's some kind of valley out here, but it's hard to get to, and I guess a lot of people don't have the time to make the effort to get there.'

'Why would Shannon head for a place like that?'

'I guess it's tactical. He never meant to hang around town.'

'You mean any town. Well, he made a mistake when he took the girl. Guess he thought he could have his cake and eat it too.'

The one thing about the reddish soil was that it made it increasingly easier to track down their prey. Around them the bluffs and spires began to tower over them and they were increasingly in shadow. It was lucky they had tracks to follow because at this point the landscape began to split off into a number of trails leading to different cave formations, any of which could have led to the couple they were seeking.

'Guess he was heading for a canyon,' said Clayton.

'I think we're just about there,' said Blaze.

They found themselves at the mouth of a canyon, the way marked out in striated bands of different shades of red, orange and yellow, worn that way by thousands of years of water erosion and the winds that howled down from the hills. The edge of the canyon was like a lip and as they tottered over this, Blaze wondered how the wagon had managed the same descent, which took them downwards in a fairly steep slope for at least fifty feet. He guessed it would just have been pure dumb luck, the horses impelled forward by the heavy thing behind them, their terror carrying them forward without a spill.

The light down here was diffused and soothing; the sky a long way above the sheer sides that would make a man giddy if he tried to look all the way up their length.

The canyon floor was not just made of plain rock. Those colours of orange, ochre and red could be seen everywhere. In addition to these, shallow pools of water existed everywhere surrounded by patches of dark green grass and even low bushes. Once or twice they could even see the odd spruce tree that had managed to get a place in loose spot of ground, managing to grow fifteen feet or more tall. The winter winds brought the heavy rains into the canyon, and since it was moist down here the water did not evaporate entirely, and where there is water there is life. They even saw clumps of pink and yellow sago lilies here and there.

'This is, well, beautiful,' said Clayton, stunned at the variety he saw around them. They could even see large yellow bees and other insects hovering around the plants and supping their nectar.

'Yep,' said Blaze in agreement, but seemingly oblivious to the scenic qualities of the place. 'They managed to get down here all right.'

'I've just been thinking,' said Clayton with a trace of uneasiness, 'what if this is one of those closed canyons and they're waiting for us?'

'We don't know that, Sheriff, and I think we can hold our own. Getting the girl from him might be a little tricky, that's all.'

The space they were in narrowed considerably so that there was just room for the two of them to ride side by side. This must have been a low point for those in the wagon, it had scraped the sides, but they need not have feared, because after a couple of hundred feet the way opened up again.

Once more their horses began to climb as they came out of the canyon. At first the two riders could not see anything, and then their eyes were met with a sight that astonished them both. They were looking sideways on at a fertile valley that stretched for miles either way. This was no mere valley; it was bounded on the far side by towering walls of rock which told them instantly why it had not been claimed from the Mexican side of the border. The rock also had the quality of sheltering this place from the worst of the wind, rain and sun that affected the rest of the region. A large river that was obviously a tributary of the Colorado meandered through the area, the water brown and sluggish, which meant that over thousands of years it had brought down the soil that had created the richness of their surroundings.

The two hot, dusty, tired and hungry men were looking at a close approximation of Paradise.

Unfortunately every paradise has to have a snake of some kind. With Adam and Eve it was the serpent that had them eat from the tree of knowledge. This valley – known in translated Mexican Spanish as 'Hidden Valley' – had its own particular member of the sidewinder family in human form. The person in question was Don Luiz Ramon Valquez who had been born with the humble name of Louie.

He had been a navigator in boats along the Colorado, and discovered the valley through a tributary that came in beneath overhanging rocks that had long been avoided by other navigators as too dangerous to risk. His boldness won through because he found this largely uninhabited spot that was just ready for picking. Since going up the river again was too dangerous, he simply sailed through and found a landing spot that connected with the main river after narrowing to a mere stream. He could not believe his luck, and soon set up an expedition to the valley along with a bunch of fellow Mexicans whom he hired with gold he managed to rob from some of the miners he encountered on the American side of the river.

He had laboured long and hard to establish what was, in effect, his own little kingdom. A few Indians lived in the same place but he soon managed to finish them off with the help of his men. At the time he had been joined by some twenty or so hardy souls, but those days were long over. Don Valquez now had over sixty *vaqueros* who answered to his every command.

He lived in what he liked to call his '*hacienda*' or house, but this building was really a small fort, built around a central square, with gates that could be lifted and lowered at will. The building was solid and foursquare on the outside with a tower at each corner. It was largely painted white, but with splashes of red, black and green around the arched windows so that they stood out like watchful eyes. One side of the fort lay beside the sluggish river and the watercourse had been artificially widened at this point to include a wide jetty.

Valquez had not just annexed the land. He had used the plains in the middle of the valley for a set purpose, and now had at least 10,000 cattle in the area. He made his money by trading his herds with suppliers in Mexico, taking the cattle downstream in flat-bottomed barges with penned in areas that he had designed especially for that purpose. He'd had plenty of time to build up his business, for he had been here for twenty years, starting after the civil war, which was one of the reasons he had fled here in the first place.

Physically he was a big, barrel-chested man with a deep voice and hair that was still black, but beginning to thin so that he plastered what was left across his pate with duck grease. He was the master of all he surveyed, until, that is, it came to the settlers.

In the years that had fallen since the valley had been discovered by the Don, there had been a great expansion across the land. The American government had encouraged – indeed they had almost forced those who lived in the east – to move outwards and annex the land, building up farms, ranches and businesses. This was all very well, but it meant that there was fierce competition amongst settlers. A certain John Kent had heard rumours about a fertile valley in the region so he had persuaded a motley group of settlers, some British by birth, other Americans, and some eastern Europeans, all of whom had decided to make their ways as pioneers to follow him to the region. They had taken some persuading, and would have rebelled against their makeshift leader if he had not found the narrow-throated Whispering Canyon by mistake and finally led them to this land of milk and honey.

The valley was over sixteen miles long and ten miles wide, with large clumps of cottonwood and mesquite trees growing near the water. This meant that even though they shared the valley with the Don who had claimed it for his own, they did not know that they had done so for over two years. In that time, the fifteen families with over a hundred members who made up the settlers established a small village with a school, a trading area, and a village hall-cum-church that was used as a communal headquarters should there ever be any kind of attack. Then they spread out and claimed an area of land each, staking down their boundaries, and began to farm to the best of their ability. They had even brought pigs, goats and cattle with them, and although many of them had died on the initial journey across the scrubland, those left soon turned into breeding populations.

The one thing the settlers did not have with them was a great deal of weaponry. Given that the Indians in the greater part of the land had been subdued a little while back, and the fact that the valley seemed so remote, there did not seem to be a great need for any kind of weapons. So the farmers had only a few guns between them and most of their bullets had run out a long time ago. This would not have mattered if they had been left alone to farm in peace. Eventually their community would have given rise to a thriving town and they would have been able to deal with the outside world and buy as many weapons as they wanted. What they did not expect was to find that they were under the rule of a master who totally ignored their right to stake a claim to the land.

Valquez was a despot; as far as he was concerned, the land was his and he had every right to do what he wanted with it, and anyone he found there.

The first thing the farmers knew about the situation was when a group of *vaqueros* came to the village and asked to speak to their leaders. They were not led by the Don himself, but by Julio Fernandez. Fernandez was not a kind man. He was in middle age and had fought in many battles both inside his country and on American soil.

'My Lord Chief Justice, Don Valquez, has learned of your presence on his land,' he told the astounded farmers during a meeting that he held in the village. 'He was displeased to find you here and minded to have you all summarily executed. I recommended that this should be his course of action. However, he has been merciful and decides that you will be able to stay.'

'That's mighty big of him seeing he ain't got any rights to this here land,' said John Kent instantly. The other farmers did not comment, noticing that the *vaqueros* who surrounded them were all heavily armed and looked quite capable of using their weapons. Fernandez ignored the interruption.

'You will continue to work the land, this is fertile land and crops are always useful. When you are harvesting your crops you will give them over to your lord and master in tribute, keeping enough to feed your families and to plant more for the seasons ahead. Anyone found to be transgressing this rule will be severely punished. They will be begging for the death that waits before I am finished with them.'

He had stayed along with his men until the farmers went back to their homes. It seemed to the settlers that all their hard work was for nothing and they were now little better than indentured servants to a powerful man, working all the hours they were given for little more than their keep. None of them wanted to leave the area where they had established a base with their families. The thought of having to start again elsewhere was too much to bear, for they had all worked hard to create their own individual, neat little homes.

There was a lot of bitterness in the air, and not surprisingly the man who had been their leader, John Kent, was now reviled in those very homes for having brought them to this place. Often he would face open hostility and once or twice there was talk of attacking him for having brought the community under the yoke of oppression. He and his wife Jane, their son and two daughters were now a tight-knit community largely known only to each other. This was a bitter pill to swallow for a proud man.

John Kent was not a man who would suffer indignity for too long. He worked in his fields, he harvested his crops and he looked after his family well, but he also brooded, and the more he brooded the more he focused on the cause of his problems. All his work and that of his family were for what? He would have to give everything over to a despot who was able to do what he wanted to them at a whim. He kept brooding, his hatred building up for the man. Never mind the *vaqueros*. John Kent had a mission.

He was going to destroy Valquez.

CHAPTER FIVE

Blaze and Clayton were tired and dusty from their long journey. The hunter cast around first before they made camp for the simple reason that he was not going to let the trail run cold. Clayton, who was a younger man, could only wonder at the stamina of the hunter.

'They went that way,' said Jubal Thorne, pointing towards the river. He followed the trail further on and they came to a bridge over the sluggish water. The bridge was made from a series of trees lashed together with ropes, then cedar planks laid over to form a flat surface. The whole thing was just big enough for the wagon to go over. Blaze looked at this construction with an expert eye.

'Cattle bridge, I've seen these before, roughly made and a bit unstable, but useful when you need to get those critters moving. Right, let's get sorted out.'

Rabbits and other game were plentiful so they soon had some fresh meat to cook over a fire. The plains on which they found themselves were broken up by clumps of cottonwood and white oak trees. They found a copse in the middle of one of the former and cooked some food over a low camp fire. They also went to the edge of the river and washed off some of the dust from the outside world. Their horses were tethered to the edge of the woods but out of sight too.

Thorne put down his bed roll and lay down.

'Going to get some shut-eye,' he proclaimed, 'be best if you did, too.'

'But they'll get away.'

'Why would they be trying to get away? That smartarse thinks he's shaken off all his pursuers. By the time we've rested and refreshed ourselves, we'll be in a fit state to get him and the girl.' Clayton could only agree with this wisdom, besides he was extremely tired, so he too rested.

They had slept for barely an hour when there was the sound of loud voices from outside the woods in which they had hidden. Blaze woke up and put his finger to his lips to warn the startled Clayton not to do anything. He crouched down low and made his way to the edge of the woods. A bunch of Mexican cowboys were making their way through the long grass at the edge of the river, a party of seven in all. They had evidently stopped to let their horses drink. Even as he watched they mounted and pounded off on their own business. Clayton, who had joined him, looked worried.

'We better watch out,' he said.

'Well said, but this isn't going to stop us.' Blaze waited until he was sure the men had gone. 'Right, we've had a little shut-eye, let's get moving now. Sooner we get this brat, sooner we get out of here.'

*

John Kent was not in a good state of mind. He had held a meeting with the other pioneers the previous day. They had been angry but had assembled out of respect for his former leadership and boredom with their lot. And maybe – just maybe their underlying thought was that he might have some sort of solution to their plight. Theirs was a simple truth. Not one of those who came to the meeting in the hall built by their own hands in the tiny hamlet wanted to be ruled by an overlord.

'This can't go on,' said Kent bluntly, looking around at the faces of those he had once called friends. 'We are under an oppressor who takes what is ours, the crops we have produced, and the goods we make with our own hands. We must take arms against this sea of troubles, or end it all and leave.'

One Iain Dorrans had made himself a spokesman for the rest. He was a gaunt man, cruel to animals and much given to imbibing his own corn whiskey.

'This is brave talk,' he said. 'We have roots here now, people roots and plant roots.'

'Exactly, that is why we must fight Valquez.'

'What with? Our bare hands?'

'Sure we have weapons; if we use our deceit and cunning real wisely we can trap some of his men, ambush them to gain their guns, ammunition and knives. We can scatter throughout this valley; ambush the *vaqueros* until their numbers are right down.'

Dorrans turned away from his former leader and spread his arms wide as he faced the fifty or so men and women who had attended the meeting.

'Listen to his words; heed them well, for he has just condemned us all to death.'

'People, if this goes on there will be nothing but death. A man under the yoke of another is no more. It is death to the soul,' said Kent.

'John,' said one of the Europeans, a man called Ivan Goresky, 'when I come here I escape so much oppression in my own country. Here I have fertile soil, food in my stomach, a good climate. This is not so bad, Valquez is not young. He dies soon, then maybe there is a chance for the rest of us.'

This seemed to be a general feeling amongst those at the meeting, even though Kent reminded them that Valquez had a son who was young and vigorous and who could turn out to be as big a despot as his father. Those present could not or would not respond to his reasoning.

'All right,' said Kent, 'the vote is carried and I have lost. Perhaps you are all correct and freedom will just happen one day. I'm sorry I wasted your time, my friends.'

Oddly enough, his desire to stand up and be counted seemed to have put him back in favour with the majority of the people present – all except for Dorrans, who seemed worried by Kent's very presence. He had good reason to be worried.

When the meeting broke up, Kent and his family went back to their farm, but he didn't stay for long. His wife spoke to him before he said he was going back to work.

'John, you did your best. We have to live here. Patience, pray, things will turn out well in the end.'

Kent agreed with his wife, clasping her the way women

wanted, then left to go back to his plough. Except, of course, he did not do this. He had left a note for her on the pillow so she would get it when he was long gone, and walked out to the fields that had once been his, that were now ruled by another and went to a clump of trees at the edge of the land. Here he discovered a parcel wrapped in oilskin. He unwrapped this and took out a Winchester rifle, checking it over for any flaws, though he did not check his mind for flaws. The sheer determination that had enabled him to get to the valley in the first place when no-one else believed it was really there was now getting him into trouble. He did not think that he should be under the yoke of some despot and these were *his* people, not those of Valquez. He got his horse and began to ride. Sixteen miles was a long way to go on foot and he wanted to get this job done.

He was going to assassinate Valquez and his eldest son.

It was still morning, despite the meeting, because like all farmers the people of Hidden Valley got up at an unearthly hour. He knew what he was doing in one respect, because he had already been planning his mission for some time. He knew the movements of his enemy.

Don Valquez was like all people in that he had his regular habits. As befitted a man who had ruled here for twenty years, he rarely got up before ten in the morning, dressed and ate a huge amount of food before going out for a hunt just after noon with his eldest son.

Life could get a little boring for a despot in that he had everything he wanted, but one thrill that had never left him was the desire to hunt the wild boars that lived in the woods around here. Moreover, he liked to go hunting with just one other. In the past it had been one of his men, but now it was his son because he wanted to give that young man the same thrills he got from the chase.

Wild pigs might have seemed a strange choice for hunting, but in actual fact they were some of the fiercest creatures around. They were small, ferocious, dark brown animals with a pair of sharp tusks, gnashing teeth and knifelike hoofs. Valquez liked to finish them off with a spear that he always took with him. He was fond of telling people about the time one of the boars, a big one by their standards, was stuck on the end of the spear but still so full of vigour, despite being mortally wounded, that it worked its way through the point of the spear and came down the shaft, still gnashing its teeth, wildly flailing hoofs that had ripped his clothing to shreds and left him bloody about the body before it expired on top of him.

'That day,' he told the listeners, 'I was lucky.'

Well, he wasn't going to be so lucky this day. The farmer turned hunter left his horse in the trees that bordered the valley and walked the rest of the way towards the hacienda. He was always surprised by the appearance of the building. There was a fertile plain, trees, bushes, cattle grazing peacefully, then suddenly this huge white fort that seemed to have sprung out of nowhere. He had already decided what he was going to do. He was going to find a vantage point overlooking the fort – not hard to do because the sides of the valley were so rocky – then he was going to shoot the two men as they rode out. He would wait for the gates to close first because they would take time to reopen.

In the note to his wife he had already told her to flee to the hills with the children. They were all old enough to go at her bidding, so it wasn't as if he had given her a difficult task. Luckily over the years, including a stint with the army, he had learned to take his time and plan for what he was going to do. He found a spot that was still amid the spruce and elm trees but that gave him a clear view of the main gate, then he waited, his mind filled with what he had to do.

He had never really considered what was going to happen to him after the leader was killed. That didn't matter anymore. He was out for revenge, plain and simple.

Then he heard the pounding of horses' hoofs from along the trail that led directly to the fort. Kent slipped further into the trees. He could not take even the slightest risk of being detected at this late stage in his plans, or would have done all this for nothing. When he thought he was well enough concealed in some green bushes, he dared to look out at the riders who were now visible on the trail. They consisted of eight men, six of them *vaqueros* who served the despot leader, but it was the other two who caught his attention. They were both men in their middle years. One was dressed in a grey jacket, jeans and a blue shirt. He had some kind of bearing of authority about him and he was an experienced rider. The other was a man in a long dusty coat, a black leather Stetson with a dark band of cloth around it. His shirt and jacket beneath this were in muted colours of brown and grey, he wore black trousers, and long boots with pointed toes, his long hair glinted a shade of copper in the sunlight. Even from a distance John Kent sensed some kind of power about the man. Then Blaze turned his head and stared directly at the undergrowth. Kent froze like a rabbit.

At least one person knew he was there.

CHAPTER SIX

What had happened was that the two men had decided to 'quarter' the area in conjunction with each other. There was a reason for this. Once they were across the river they discovered that there was a distinct set of marks where the wagon had moved parallel to the banks. This seemed an odd thing to do until they found that this particular trail led into the woodland that spanned either side of the water.

'Seems a strange way to proceed,' said Clayton. 'I mean they can't have wanted to set up house in the area near the plains, too easy for them to be tracked down.'

'Let's get in there and find out,' said Blaze laconically. They dismounted and hitched their horses to the nearest low branch of elder, then walked together into the woods. Once there, they found that the wagon had been unhitched and left deep enough in the woods that it would not have been discovered unless they had been searching actively for it.

'Looks like they unhitched their horses and made off that way,' said Clayton, pointing to the entrance of the woods. 'They could be anywhere in this valley.'

'That seems like the case,' said Blaze thoughtfully. He was not finished with the wagon. Instead he looked inside. Just as he thought, it was completely empty. He considered this for a short while.

'You know what? I don't think they just unhitched and rode off, I reckon they came back here a few times. That Shannon feller you were talking about seems to have planned this for a while.'

'So, why couldn't they just have ridden off?'

'There was the loot for one thing, that there bag would not have been light with the best part of $50,000 in it. Then there was the food he brought, clothing, whatever else. He planned for the long stay.'

'I still don't get what you're driving at.'

'Don't you see, Sheriff? That means they must've come back a few times. I can't see Shannon wanting to ride back from the other end of the valley four or five times.'

'I get it, so you're saying they must be nearby?'

'I'll say even more than that, I guess they must be in the hills across this side of the river.'

'What do you think we should do then?'

'I say we ride apart from a point we've both decided then look for their trail and meet up with what we've found. You know the signs by now. It also means when we've located them real well, you and I can decide on how we take Shannon. Clayton, you're going to be mighty useful!'

'Thanks,' mumbled Clayton, not sure if the hunter was being sarcastic or not.

They went to the edge of the woods facing the hills.

The mesquite and cottonwoods thrived near the water but thinned out so that there was a fairly extensive stretch of plains country between here and the hills.

The hills themselves were not bare, their slopes being covered in a mixture of spruce, pinion, and cottonwood trees. White oaks grew at the edge of the woodlands at the foot of the hills, while in between the trees grew different varieties of bushes. Not that they were able to make out much detail at this point, because the edge of the valley was some miles away from the river and the plain undulated like waves making plain view of the hills impossible. The natural folds in the landscape were probably the reason why Shannon and his willing captive had not been spotted by the *vaqueros*. Closer to the edge of the slopes lay huge rocks that had rolled down there when the valley was formed. These were black in colour, indicating that they were volcanic in origin, sticking up as if they had grown suddenly out of the earth, but were surrounded by grass.

Clayton and Blaze parted outside the woodland and did the quartering required to survey the area as quickly as possible. It was Blaze who picked up on the marks of the horses that had not been totally eliminated from the grasslands. He marked where they were then called on Clayton to join him. Clayton could not believe they had been lucky so quickly. He told his companion this.

'This is not a matter of luck,' said Blaze bluntly, 'more a matter of knowledge and ability. All we've got to do is get to where that miscreant is hiding and flush him out. You handy with that thing at your side?'

'I can shoot,' said Clayton a little coldly. Like most

people faced with someone who did not really care, he felt as if he was being ordered around. As one who was used to lording it over Mikey, he did not like the feeling when it was thrown back at him.

They rode towards the woodlands at the outer edge of the plain. Both men were aware of a feeling of relief. This business would be over by midday. The trip back to El Frontera then Harrisville would be taxing, but they would have achieved their aim. Neither of them even contemplated the thought of being killed.

As the trees came into sight they became aware of the thundering of horses behind them. This was not the two refugees they were looking for, that became plain enough. Seven horsemen were riding across the plain in a purposeful manner. Blaze thought back to when he had called out to Clayton not that long ago. The *vaqueros* must have heard him. He cursed his lack of caution for not thinking of attracting their attention. His mind had been too fixed on getting Shannon and the girl.

They could have tried to flee from the approaching horsemen, but some of them were armed with long rifles. In addition their horses were magnificent stallions equipped with the high Mexican saddles, with blankets underneath to pad their impact on the back of the horses. These were men who spent most of the day in the saddle and covered large distances easily and as comfortably as if they were in a large chair at home. Blaze felt as if his own hardy quarter-horse was suddenly inadequate, while Clayton's roan was just an average specimen of the type. Whatever else they were, neither of the two men lacked courage. They turned their mounts to face the approaching *vaqueros* and waited.

Their leader was a big man with one of the most ferocious moustaches either of them had ever seen. It curled up on either side of his face spreading beyond the boundaries of his features. Below this bristling defence he had a large, cruel mouth while above, his eyes were fierce, piggy and not unlike those of the wild boar his master Valquez liked to go hunting. He looked at the newcomers with some degree of contempt.

'Who are you? What do you want here? I should kill you.'

'We are visitors, my name is Jubal Thorne and this is Sheriff Dan Clayton. Isn't that right, Sheriff?'

'Yes.'

'Many people know where we are, because we told them where we were going,' said Thorne. He knew that in all probability he could take all seven of these men who did not know what a ferocious fighting machine they were facing, however, it had long been his policy not to engage in combat unless it was strictly necessary and this was one of those times. He had to impress upon this man how important his mission was, and he had to do it fast. 'Forgive me, who am I addressing?'

'I am Raul Fernandez,' said the leader of the *vaqueros*. 'I am the second-in-command of our glorious leader, Don Valquez. You are intruding upon his land.'

'For that we beg your forgiveness, but we are here for a reason.'

'What is that reason? I would hear you out.'

'A bad man has come to this oasis in the middle of waste.

He is so bad that he hurt women and children for the greed of money. Worse even than that, he has taken a young girl and he has made off with her. Are you a father?'

'Yes, I have four children all who live within the valley.'

'Is one of them a girl?'

'Two of them girls, they are fine daughters. One day they will go back to the motherland and marry well.'

'Can you imagine how you would feel if one of them was taken from you? Well, that is how her father feels. That young girl is in danger.'

Clayton had an alarmed look on his face, he thought that Blaze was telling Fernandez too much, but Thorne gave his new friend a reassuring glance. Clayton shrugged his shoulders and relaxed a little, making his features stony. If they could find a way out of this without having to battle for their lives he was happy.

'I would kill that man who took my Conchita.'

'Well, her father feels no differently. Now you will understand why we are here, this is our mission.'

'So where are they?'

This was a crucial turning point in the conversation and Thorne knew this full well. He was not about to reveal to this man that he knew how to track down the criminal. This Fernandez had a treacherous bearing, he could very well turn on them like a ferocious dog and cut them down once they revealed where Shannon was hiding and take the reward for his own.

'That is something we do not know just yet. Once we have him within our grasp we will take him back to Harrisville where he will hang for his crimes. If we can capture him alive that is.' Thorne had not lied once. He did not really know Shannon's location at that moment and he had been asked to bring the criminal back dead or alive. He had discovered the power of truth a long time ago. It was possible to use truth in such a way that it was far more effective than any lie.

'May I ask you a favour?'

'You may ask, stranger.'

'Can we speak to your commander-in-chief? We would rather proceed with his full permission and the help of your men than be out here without anyone to look after our backs.' Thorne's horse shifted a little as he said these words and his hair moved aside, revealing some of his ruined features. One or two of the men drew their own mounts back and he heard Fernandez give a sharp intake of breath.

'You, with the ruined face, I have heard something of you, even here. We trade with our cattle and crops; we speak to the outside world.' He paused for thought and Thorne knew that this was a crucial moment in his relations with these men. Fernandez was a big, cruel man, used to taking what he wanted. 'Very well, you may go with these men and meet with Don Valquez. You can tell him your story and see if you can enlist his help. At the very least you will provide a change of diet for the dogs.'

Clayton turned pale at this taunting humour, but the *vaqueros* laughed heartily at their leader's joke. Some of the laughter seemed a little forced to Thorne and he realized these were cowboys who had a job to do. They were not as warlike as they appeared with their long rifles and bullet-belts. Fernandez was the one to worry about.

'Lead on, MacDuff,' said Blaze, quoting his favourite author.

'I lead nowhere,' said Fernandez. He turned to his *vaqueros*. 'Take these men to see Don Valquez. If they try to escape, shoot them down and leave their corpses out as a warning to anyone who would defy us.'

'Wait, you're not coming with us?'

'I have work to do, a cattle drive coming up, men to supervise. Once these ones have escorted you out they will come back to me.' With that he rode off on his huge mount.

The other *vaqueros* surrounded the visitors. They did not speak English as well as their leader, but simply indicated from their movements where the new arrivals had to go. The ride to the other end of the valley took over an hour and like anyone else, they were astonished by the big white building on the hill that seemed so out of place in this lush valley. As they came closer to the place their fate would be determined, Blaze had a sense that someone was watching them. His survival instincts had been honed by years of being a man hunter. He turned his head as they were escorted through the gate. Someone was waiting for a kill; he sensed that electric aura in the air. He could bring this to the attention of his escort, and then he decided not to bother. He and Clayton already had enough on their plate. He turned and looked stolidly ahead, his mind in turmoil as the drawbridge was lowered to let them into Don Valquez's fortress home.

CHAPTER SEVEN

The cabin was up in the hills above Hidden Valley. It had been built some time ago, constructed from the local wood; the wood was properly overlapped and caulked with moss and dried clay against the weather. Even so, it was an old building and had holes in the roof. The interior was musty with the smell of damp. There was a pot-bellied stove in the corner atop of which stood a greasy griddle. The furnishings were not extensive, consisting of two wooden chairs, one of which was quite rickety and a table that had not been wiped in a long time.

Their bedding lay in opposite corners because Shannon was slightly prudish with regard to their sleeping arrangements. As far as he was concerned this was the woman he loved and he had to treat her so accordingly until they were married. The room also had a low chest with a hasp and a padlock. The chest had already been there, and it was where he deposited the precious load from the robbery. In that chest was his – sorry – *their* future. He did not know yet how he was going to tell her that he was going to keep the money. They would find a way around that problem in the future.

When they reached the shack with the tinned food, the bedding, lamps, oil and everything else they could carry, Shannon promptly asked the girl to come back to the wagon with him and help get as many other supplies as possible before they had time to make the place halfway presentable. He had apologized for making her work so hard. In this he had underestimated her. Alice Lovell may have been the lady of the manor, but she was no stranger to hard work. She helped out with the Mission in town and cooked for and fed the unfortunates who drifted through there from time to time. She was also an able manager for her father who often suffered bouts of debilitating fatigue and often carried out his orders by proxy, riding to the mines and seeing they were carried out. This meant she was no shrinking violet when it came to cleaning up the shack and storing away their provisions.

From time to time she caught Shannon looking at her with open admiration and found she was thinking how much she loved him, and wanted to be with him. This was not a feeling that was to last for long.

They settled in and ate some fried eggs and bread. This, along with the coffee he brewed atop the stove, tasted like nectar to her after all the ordeals they had been through to get there.

'Guess we'll just stay here awhile until the roarin' dies down,' he said across the rough table at which they were both seated.

'I'm happy with that,' said the girl. 'This place is really

beautiful. Why, we've even got a stream of crystal water flowing down from the hills not too far away from the hut. We could be happy enough here for a while.'

'We sure could,' he said, giving her a genuine smile that warmed her heart. 'Trouble is, if we stay here we're going to need some fresh meat.'

'That's all right then, River, I'll come out and go hunting with you.'

'No, can't be that way.' He stood up as he shook his head with regret. Amongst the many accoutrements he had with him were various bits of rope. One of these was made of leather and while he was talking he had been making it into a loop. She had assumed this was something to do with the horses, but she could not have been more wrong. With a swiftness that argued he had done this kind of thing before he went behind her, grabbed her right hand and slid the loop on to her wrist, pulled it through the rods at the back of her chair, looped it around her other arm and pulled it tight. He turned the leather around her upper arms a few more times; securing it against the back of the chair before he was satisfied that she was a prisoner. She would have kicked out, but she was facing the low table and this blocked her movements. With the strength in his young body he turned the chair around so that it was facing the door, then walked around to face her at enough of a distance to avoid any attempt she might make to kick out at him.

The events had taken just a few seconds, had been so swift that the girl hardly knew yet what had happened.

'Let me go!' she screamed, tightening her arms against

her bonds and feeling them bite into her tender young flesh, her firm breasts straining towards him as she did so. When these words produced no effect she gave vent to a loud scream. This was seemingly too much for him, he leaned over and slapped her hard across the face, and she tried to bite his hand. He stepped back. She was glaring at him now.

'Listen here, Alice, I got to get meat and mebbe see a few people, settlers who can help us out. You got to stay here and I could see you wasn't about to do that. What's a man got to do?' He didn't mention the fact that he didn't trust anyone with the dollars he had put in the chest.

'Bastard!' she hissed.

'Look, this ain't paradise we're in. There's some real bad people out there who'd do you in soon as they look at you. I'm doing this for your own good. I love you, Alice, but it's got to be on my terms if we're gonna make a go of it.'

She began to scream again.

'Right, you asked for this.' He tied a bandana across her mouth. She tried to spit it out, but his touch was sure and firm as he slid the cloth between her plump lips. He stood back and looked at her with real regret.

'I needed to bring you here, Alice, and we can make this work if we try. Be away a couple of hours, that's all.' He picked up his gun and went out of the cabin without looking back.

She was not her father's girl for nothing. He may have thought that she was the kind of person who would just sit there passively and wait for him but that wasn't for her. Maybe he was right about the danger out there, and yes she would have insisted on going with him, but that didn't mean he had to treat her like a prisoner. With this in mind she sat and did something that he had underestimated her ability to do. She sat and thought about how she was going to get out of here.

There was nothing wrong with her eyesight and by straining her neck, she lighted on the knife she had been using to cut up the bread. It had a long, serrated blade, a black wooden handle. With this thought in mind she began to push her chair back towards the table. Her long shapely legs flexing as she strained against the rough wooden floorboards, her breasts straining against the fabric of her blouse. She had to be careful or she would end up tipping the chair over and all she would achieve would be to end up lying on the floor like a trussed chicken, helpless until the return of the man whom she now hated with all her heart.

Inch by agonizing inch she moved the chair until she had it positioned in such a way that she had access to the table, had maneuvered it in such a way that she was facing the wall with the table behind her. She had long, slim fingers and had often played the piano for her father. She had even played the same instrument for Shannon that first night when she decided she loved him more than anyone else in the world. Now a strangled sob escaped from her lips as she groped for the handle of the knife. A couple of times she managed to touch the handle but it was that little bit out of reach. If her mouth had not been gagged she would have screamed with frustration. At last she held the handle and managed to turn the knife to her bonds. She was sawing at the rope that held her upper left arm. Once or twice she caught her own flesh and could feel the blood run down. Finally she managed to snag the leather and saw away more firmly. At last the tough material parted and she felt the rope fall partly away.

Another ten minutes passed before she was able to free herself completely. The last thing she did was remove the red bandana and spit on it before throwing it into a corner. Uppermost was the idea that she had to get some kind of help to get away from here. The cabin was situated in the middle of a wooded slope and could not be seen from below, Shannon had left the horses amid the oaks at the bottom of the hill where the ground levelled out but they still could not be seen. One of the sturdy little mustangs was still tied up there, the saddle to one side. The girl threw on the saddle and tightened the cinch straps. She was going to get help.

The sun was now up considerably and the day was hot as she rode out onto the plain beside the wooded slopes. She headed towards the wooden cattle bridge over the sluggish river. Not knowing the valley, nor the direction Shannon had taken, she was about to head towards the settlement without knowing it was there, where she would have been fairly safe, when she heard loud voices coming from the large clump of cottonwood trees beside the river. She saw a bunch of big, fine-looking horses tied up outside the copse. Cattle were milling around in the middle distance, a fact that surprised her.

Normally she would have exercised some degree of caution in approaching such a group, but she was so furious at her treatment at the hands of her former lover that she did not want to let a second pass. She got off her mount and left him beside the other horses while she went to the source of the noise.

There in the woodland sat a group of *vaqueros* around a campfire. The woodland was cool and slightly damp, the light filtering through the leaves giving the scene a green tinge. The men had taken off their sombreros, laid their weapons against trees – for who would attack them here? – and were cooking the remains of a wild pig. They wore linen shirts, black trousers, and were evidently working men who were taking a break from driving the herds of cattle to their destination; they numbered seven in all.

They looked up as the girl appeared.

'Help me,' she said. 'I was brought here but I've changed my mind now. I need to get home. There will be a reward.'

The men all got to their feet, unsure of what to do, but one man who was young, with overlong slicked back hair and bolder than the rest, looked the girl over. He paid no attention to her words but looked at her body with the air of a predator.

'My father will give you a good reward,' said the girl.

The young man made a remark in Spanish to the others. One or two laughed, but the rest looked worried. The young man reached out a long dirty hand and stroked her cheek. She pulled back.

'My father …' she began, just as the young man reached forward and seized her, pressing his body against hers.

She could feel his arousal straight away. She wasted no more time in speaking but raked her nails across his dark features, and then as he let her go with a muffled curse, she turned and began to run, only to sprawl on the ground, her skirt riding around her waist as he put out a foot and tripped her. It was obvious what was going to happen next.

Two of the men were holding back, looking worried but the other five were willing to go ahead and carry out their brutal act on the seemingly helpless woman. Then there was a hoarse cry and her attacker was pushed aside by a big man with a bristling moustache who strode into the clearing, uttering a hoarse phrase in Spanish. The girl scrabbled backwards on the ground, pushing with her feet, feeling the coarse surface and thorns bite into the palms of her hands as the two men argued. She was just about to rise when the moustachioed man gave a brutal laugh and flung some words to his men over his shoulder and all of them laughed, some a little doubtfully. It seemed that the argument had simply been about who was going to take the girl first and it was obvious that this man was the leader. He was better-dressed than the rest, his clothes made of finer material and it was obvious he looked on the girl as a little light diversion sent from heaven until he could get on with his day. When they were finished with her they would simply kill her and hide her body in the woods. Her situation was dire.

Just as the big man was unbuttoning his trousers there was an inarticulate cry from the undergrowth. The man lifted his head. There was the crack of a bullet that did not miss its target. It hit the moustachioed man right between the eyes, leaving a fairly small hole at the front but blowing out the back of his head. He gave a cry and toppled backwards to the ground, his hands still on his flies, dead.

The other *vaqueros* fumbled for their weapons, while the girl was so startled by the events transpiring in front of her eyes that she remained on the ground. This was probably the best place for her. Within five minutes the men were decimated by an invisible enemy who skirted the copse and shot them one by one with an accuracy that killed each of them at the first shot. This was not someone who had just arrived; it was an observer who had been there for some time and knew what he was doing.

When the first three were killed there was a general rout as the rest tried to rush out of the clearing. They were shot in the back, one after the other as they tried to flee. One luckless victim tripped over the body of the man in front and had the back of his head blown off as he tried to rise. The gunshots finished and there was an eerie silence in that clearing, broken only by the desperate panting of the girl. She was going to die for nothing. She should have remained tied up where she was.

Nothing happened, she was left alive.

Then a slim, tall figure stepped into the green copse, still holding an army Colt in each hand, the ones capable of shooting extra bullets. It was River Shannon and he looked extremely angry. For a second he pointed one of the guns at her head and in that moment she thought he was going to kill her there and then. She scrabbled to her feet. She was no longer resentful of this man, she was afraid, deadly afraid, and for a good reason since she had seen what he was capable of doing.

'I thought I left you tied up.'

'You did,' she said, trying to remain defiant. 'I used my

wits to escape.'

'You didn't use your wits enough.'

'I thought they were going to help me.'

'Help you? These men sure ain't looking to give you handouts. This is a place where they can do pretty much whatever they want and that includes raping a pretty girl who don't know what she's doing.'

'How did you find me?'

'I saw the horses, heard you cry out and figured it out. Just as I hid my horse and came in to get you, that one arrived.' He indicated the first man he had shot. 'Can't say I'm sorry to have done away with that one, he's never been someone I liked.'

'You know him?'

'Sure, his name's Fernandez. He brought me here two years ago when I helped him with some trading down the river and into Mexico. Turned out he wanted to recruit fresh blood for that Don of his. That didn't suit me, to become the servant of a servant, so I jumped it off into the hills.' His eyes were slightly glazed and he spoke almost absently. He shook his head as if to clear his gaze and seemed to see the corpses he had created for the first time. The flies were already beginning to make inroads, buzzing around the fresh meat.

'You don't know what you've done here.'

'Me? I haven't done anything!'

'Yes, you have, if you'd stayed put none of this would have happened. I ought to kill you too.' He pointed the guns at her head, thought better of the act and holstered them. 'Can you even comprehend what you've done? This man lying here ain't just some feller called Fernandez. He's the right-hand man of the guy who runs this place. What I've just done is start a war. The Don won't let an insult like this lie, he's like all his people, he believes in blood revenge.'

'We could go and see him, explain everything, say he was about to dishonour me.'

Shannon stepped forward and the girl could smell the odour of his sweat. His young features were contorted with rage as he pushed his hard body against hers. Yet she could feel his arousal and was frightened he was going to carry out the very act he had prevented from the others. He seized her face, his calloused fingers pressing hard.

'You get back on the horse and we go to the cabin and wait this out. OK?'

She nodded, unable to speak as she gazed into the eyes of a killer.

CHAPTER EIGHT

As the horsemen rode into the fort, they heard the rattle of loose boards when the drawbridge leading to the building was drawn up behind them. They passed over great flat paving slabs of grey stone hewn from the hills around them, then under a central arch until they were into the building.

Their horses were now in a main square with coloured paving picked out like a chessboard, but in red and blue, beneath the restless hoofs of their mounts. In front of them and either side the floors of the building raised three stories high. This did not seem like much, but since some of the rooms below were above average height so they could host functions, the second and third floors were high above their heads. Clayton looked all round, taking in as much as he could as if he was going to write it down afterwards. Mostly just to conceal his nervousness at their situation.

But Blaze only gave his surroundings a cursory glance to make sure no other gunmen were on guard. Once he made sure of this, he looked at the man who was sitting on the white wickerwork chair at the courtyard, being fanned by a young girl with a palm leaf to keep him cool.

The appointed leader of the *vaqueros* got off his horse and spoke rapidly in Spanish to the man in the chair. The man answered him back just as rapidly. Then he turned to the two new arrivals.

'Get off your horses and talk to our leader.'

Blaze dismounted, as did Clayton and the two men approached the chair. Don Valquez was not at all what they had expected. They had pictured him as a tall, commanding man with blunt granite features and white hair who was used to everyone following his barked orders. What they got instead was a plump, rather jolly-looking man who had all his side hair which was black rather than grey, and who was a little bald on top. His rotund body was made more so by his tight white cotton shirt, red cummerbund, and black trousers, and shiny leather boots.

He looked as fresh as a daisy despite the heat of the day and was ultra-clean beside his dirty and sweaty men. He had a few gaps in his teeth as he spoke but a man could not reach sixty without a few losses of this kind.

'Welcome, gents,' he said, 'it is so long since visitors came to this place. To what is owed this unexpected pleasure?'

'I guess your man might have told you,' said Blaze tartly.

'I am Don Luiz Valquez,' said the leader amiably enough. 'You were sent to me by Joachim Fernandez, my second-in-command in these parts.'

'You are a Commander? But you are not at war here,' said Blaze.

'War is what you have been to in the past and I might in the future.' For a moment the mask slipped and he revealed his true nature with a steely look and a cruel thinning of his mouth. 'But that is a matter for when it arises. Can you give me an account of yourselves?'

'Yep, I'm Jubal Thorne, also known as Blaze,' said the man hunter promptly. 'Your turn, Dan.'

'I am Dan Clayton, Sheriff of El Frontera.' There was a stirring from the Don at this.

'El Frontera? I have been to this place in my youth. It was a small town at the time, arising from a trading station on the way to my homeland. Yet you are here now. This seems a strange thing to me.' He looked at Blaze with experienced eyes. 'You are a man who is not always on the side of law.'

'Not always,' admitted Blaze in his lazy voice.

'So why are you here that I should not have you killed for violating my land?' The words were said in such an easy way that the full impact of his words sank in slowly.

'I think you might want to hear us out on that one,' said Blaze. 'We've got a job to do here and we just want to get on with it.'

'He's right,' said Clayton. 'This here miscreant, a man who knows this place broke the law real bad, and fled here.'

'I can understand why the hunter, but why a sheriff?'

'He brought trouble to my town,' said Clayton. He spoke in a guarded manner and suddenly Blaze realized he did not want to talk about the girl to this man. Blaze immediately understood why. If he let them know there was an heiress in the valley the Don would immediately see how he could make money out of her. He would also try to use the sheriff as an envoy for contacting her father.

80

'So you need to get the bad man?' The Don gave a mocking laugh and looked at them through narrow, piggy, boar-like eyes. 'There is something you're not telling me. If you want help from me, tell the truth. Tell it now.'

Blaze became aware that the other *vaqueros* had dismounted and were at their backs. This was not a problem for Blaze because he knew that he could pull the guns out of his deep pockets, do a roll and get all of them before they could get him – he had that much confidence in his abilities, but he was not so sure about Clayton. The sheriff was an older man and a little ponderous; he might find it difficult to move fast in that kind of situation. Blaze looked directly into the eyes of the man who would decide their fate in here.

'There's money involved.'

'How much money.'

'A lot?'

'What is a lot of money?'

'Over $50,000, barring what his men spent in that whorehouse and hotel in El Frontera.'

Blaze spoke so directly and so sincerely that the Don could not help being impressed.

'That truly is a lot of money, my friend.' He gave the matter small thought. 'I give you permission to do this hunt.'

'That is good of you, Don Valquez,' said Blaze. 'We thank you for your kindness from the bottom of our hearts.'

'Now go,' said the Don. 'Find this miscreant and take him to your justice. I want nothing to do with him. Let me know when he is caught. Do you want my men to help you?'

'No, it might alarm him if too many pursue him and he might go to ground. Again, I thank you.'

The Don settled back and the young lady began to fan him again. It was obvious that the audience was over.

The two men mounted their horses and began to leave the courtyard. Some of the *vaqueros* were about to follow but their leader barked a short command at them. This time only two horses left over the open bridge. When they were gone Valquez turned to his man Pepe, who had led them here. He spoke in his native language.

'Make sure that Fernandez keeps an eye on them and that when they find the money, he has them dispatched and the fortune brought here.'

'You are already rich, Commander, is it worth bringing the wrath of the outside authorities down on your head?'

'That may be so, but I have a feeling those authorities don't even know where they have tracked down this evildoer. And Pepe, dead men tell no tales.'

Once they were out of the fort that was also a giant hacienda, Clayton seemed to breathe a little easier.

'That went quite well,' he said, turning his head to his new friend.

'You think so?'

'You don't?'

'Why didn't you mention the girl?'

'I had a feeling it wouldn't be wise.'

'When Fernandez comes back he'll spill the truth.'

'I'm hoping we'll be gone by then.'

'Say, that conversation could've easily gone either way.

Do you think that old rogue built up his little empire by being nice to all and sundry?'

'He did not seem all that threatening.'

'Why should he? Are you really so foolish as to think he would do his dirty work on his own? Those men were ready to take us out at a droop of his eyelids. Why do you think I had my hands in my pockets the whole time?'

'To keep 'em warm? All right, I get it.'

They rode on in silence for a short while then Blaze raised his head and sniffed the air like an old hound dog tracing a scent.

'Follow me over to the wooded slopes,' he said.

'What in the blue heavens are you planning now?'

'Just do it.'

Such was the overwhelming personality of the man that the sheriff obeyed against his better judgement. By this time they were about quarter a mile from the fort. Blaze tied his tether to a tree limb.

'Wait here, don't move,' he told Clayton in a low voice, and then he was off in the undergrowth and soon lost to sight.

He was going by a highly tuned instinct that told him there was danger in these woods. Some men would ignore such feelings of disquiet and ride on, but several times in his life he had experienced the same thoughts and acting on them had saved his life. He tracked his way through the woodland, his experienced eye picking up the traces of the man who had gone before him. He did not waste much time on his quest because there, close to the fort now, but hidden well in the woodland, was the object of his search.

He turned out to be a man in his thirties with short sandy hair, a dark brown shirt, and long britches who even from behind looked like the farmer he was. Blaze stole silently to a point where he was close behind the man and delivered a swift, paralyzing blow to the man's shoulder. The recipient gave a cry of pain and dropped his weapon, which Blaze instinctively kicked down the slope into some bushes.

'What in the name of hellfire …' The man spun around and flailed out with his good arm but Blaze had already anticipated this and had stepped out of his range.

The farmer was about to offer more violence, only stopping short when he saw he was looking down the short twin barrels of the Peacemakers that Blaze had swiftly pulled out of his pockets.

Blaze saw that the man was gaunt and unshaven, with deep hollows beneath his eyes indicating that he had not slept for a long time. This was the face of a fanatic and Blaze had dealt with this kind of person, both religious and otherwise to know that this was someone who might not be entirely persuaded by reason.

'Jubal Thorne's the name,' he said amiably enough. 'Who the heck are you, stranger?'

'John Kent.' The man stiffened his back defiantly even though he was trembling all over, more from fatigue than fear. 'You sure did a number on my arm.' He clutched at that appendage. 'You bloody ugly traitor,' he added as the gunman's long hair swung loose and he saw the disfiguring scars, hatred making an ugly scowl out of his own usually good features.

'I'm going to let that one go for now,' said Blaze evenly,

'considering you're under some kind of distress. But I've got to ask why you're here in the first place.'

'I was going to blow your head off when I saw you,' said Kent. 'I thought you knew then, on the way in. But I've got a higher job, to get that tyrant and his brat and shoot them in the head.'

'You're a mighty ambitious man.'

'I would've nailed them too, just as they came out of the gates.'

'Wait a minute; doesn't Valquez go out with the protection of his men?'

'Nope, he goes hunting with his eldest whelp, just the two o' them, predictable as winter rain. Every day 'bout the same time. It was just a matter of waiting.' His face contorted with anger again. 'And you had to come along and spoil it all.'

'Listen to me, Kent, I'm no expert in your local politics. But I say you have to get more weapons, persuade whoever lives alongside you to unite, and fight them that way. Do you have a wife and children?' Caught by the aura of the man Kent nodded wordlessly. 'Then let me tell you, if you killed Valquez and his heir they would have taken a blood oath to rid the valley of your people. Is that what you want, my friend, your wife and children to be hunted down and exterminated like vermin?'

'You're right.' Kent sat down and covered his face with his hands. 'I thought my family could hide in the hills, but the *vaqueros* and the leaders know this entire valley. I was about to condemn a lot of innocent people to death.' He sat like that for a few seconds then looked around for his rifle. 'Guess I should end it now and save a lot of people the trouble.'

'For a moment there I thought I was going to have to do the job for you.' Blaze put his guns away, confident there was going to be no shooting now.

'Maybe I should have let you.'

'I don't want to hear this anymore. There's a lot of hope for you. You just have to strike at the right time.'

'Why should I believe you? You were in there conferring with that demon less than half an hour ago, then you came out with your buddy. Looks to me as if you're well in with him.'

'Listen, we were brought here by an escort of his men, believe you me we have better things to do, we have our own quarry to seek. I'm about as much on his side as you are. Now are you going along with this or are you going to do something stupid? I have a lot of business to do and I ain't hanging around.'

'I'll go home,' said Kent simply, 'but I'm coming with you first.'

'Why?' Blaze was genuinely surprised at this.

'Because you kinda know what you're doing and you know about weapons. Looks to me as if sticking by your side's the right thing to do for the moment.'

'OK, meet us about quarter a mile back if that's what you want.' Blaze left and returned to Clayton, who seemed relieved at the appearance of his friend.

'I thought you had gone nuts, taking off like that.'

'Well, here's the evidence,' said Blaze.

Kent, having thought the matter over, arrived on his

mount a minute or so later. He introduced himself.

'Kent is sticking with us awhile,' said Blaze, 'he doesn't quite trust his ability to go back into the bosom of his family.'

'Do you know why we're here?' asked Clayton.

'Nope,' said Kent.

'Well, ride with us and I'll fill you in on the way there,' said the sheriff. 'Guess you'll be useful, you'll know the lie of the land better than us anyway, you might be able to show us where to go. Plus three against one, even if that one is a known killer, seems like pretty good odds to me.'

He did not know how wrong he could be.

The three horsemen rode off together.

CHAPTER NINE

'If they went to the area near the cattle bridge there's only one place they could have gone,' said Kent, having heard the whole story.

'There's a cabin up on the slopes amongst the trees. Belonged to an old hermit who'd found this place long before any of us. Built it with his own two hands. I've used it when I've been out hunting.'

'So you can lead us straight there?'

'Yep.' Kent was a man of few words, but he kept his word when he got them to dismount near the foot of the slopes on the other side from the canyon that had brought the two visitors to the valley.

As they tethered their horse, Blaze noticed something right away that none of his companions remarked upon. Clayton took out his dogleg firearm as they climbed towards the old shack, while Blaze took out his Peacemakers. Kent was holding his Winchester in one hand and grabbing at branches with the other to help his climb. He was eager for action, having been thwarted so badly earlier that day.

Blaze counselled him in a low voice to hold back because the man was behaving in a manner that was calculated to get his head blown off. Kent did not seem to mind the thought all that much.

Blaze was resigned to whatever was going to happen but he just knew that whatever else they were going to do, they would have to try and rescue the girl.

The door of the cabin was open, wide to the world. Four dead quail, the same number of equally dead rabbits lay at the entrance.

Blaze immediately holstered his guns and strode towards the building.

'If that place is occupied, it'll be your turn to get your blamed head shot off, going out like that,' said Kent.

'Don't think so.' Blaze went into the cabin, which was completely empty, the other two following close behind. They took in the scene, the knife that lay on the floor, the sundered leather that had once held Alice tied to the old chair. Blaze inspected the rope. 'Just as I thought, this was sawed in two by this knife. Looks as if he trussed her up and went off to do some hunting, came back and found she wasn't here.'

'Then he threw his kill down and went to find her,' said Clayton.

'I guessed neither of them would be here when I arrived,' said Blaze. 'The clue was in the fact that we didn't see their horses just where I would have expected to find them.'

'Guess we'll have to leave this dead end, or wait for them to come back,' said Clayton.

'Shannon might come back, but I seriously doubt if we'll

see the girl here again,' said Blaze. He looked around the cabin for where the money might have been hidden. He saw an empty chest and realized that was where it had been concealed. No more. He walked out of the empty building shaking his head.

In some senses Kent seemed disappointed that he had not been able to vent his anger on the missing outlaw. Clayton was not sure about the man, he seemed like a simmering volcano that was about to blow its top.

By then it was getting towards mid-afternoon. Their horses had been quietly cropping at the grass and resting, so they were quite refreshed when the three men came back to get them.

'Reckon your outlaw probably headed for the woods that break up the plains,' said Kent. He looked thoughtful. 'Those are the very woods that stopped Valquez knowing about our settlement and the other way round too. Wish it had stayed that way,' he added savagely.

The other two, lacking direction, agreed with him. The trail was so confusing it was hard even for Blaze to get his bearings.

They rode across the grassy plain together, the hot sun beating down on their backs. They came upon the several hundred cattle who had settled down near the woodland. They were big, beige longhorns in their summer coats. Kent stared at the herd.

'This ain't right,' he said. 'By all accounts there should be a bunch of *vaqueros* out here to deal with them. In fact, they should've been gone by now, considering they're going to market.'

'I see you keep up with your enemy,' said Clayton.

'Yup,' answered Kent, 'it's the best way to avoid 'em.'

When they came closer to the woodland down from the cattle bridge, they saw that a bunch of fine big horses were tethered in front of a well-worn entrance to the woods. Kent turned to his new friends. 'Guess something's gone wrong here.'

Blaze knew too that this was not a normal way for matters to proceed. For a start there should have been someone to guard the herd, although he could see why normal precautions might be suspended in a place like Hidden Valley where one man ruled and they had no enemies. This time Blaze tugged back his long, heavy hair, the sun catching glints off the copper tones, lifting up his eye patch to reveal his staring eye.

Clayton, who had seen him like this before, still reacted with a startled glance, but Kent stared blatantly at the hunter as if seeing some kind of demon being unleashed amongst them.

Blaze ignored his companions, took both guns out of his pockets, and advanced along the well-worn trail into the woodland. It seemed as if this was a place where the *vaqueros* had talked and eaten with each other for many years. The other two took out their weapons too, and then followed him into the glade where the *vaqueros* usually spent their time. The only sounds that could be heard were their footsteps rustling against the undergrowth, the chattering of the birds high up in the leaves above them, and the restless buzzing of a million insects.

Men lay everywhere in the positions in which they had

been killed. The stench of corrupting blood and ruptured intestines filled the air. What had once been a lovely forest glade where a man could have some rest and food had been turned into a scene of horror and deadly devastation. While the other two stood there, too stunned by what they were taking in to move, Blaze pocketed his guns and strolled over to the bodies as if he was taking a walk in the park. He turned them over one by one if they had fallen on their faces. He did not have to do this with the last one, who was a big man with a black, curled moustache that looked somewhat pathetic on his fat face now that he had a bullet hole in his head.

'Hey, Kent, recognize this one?' he asked.

Kent came over and stared down at the man with a glint in his normally sombre eyes.

'Son, I wish I'd done this one myself.'

'Take it you know him?'

'Yup, that's Fernandez, calls himself the lieutenant of them *vaqueros*. Never fought a real war in his life.'

'Is that so? Care to tell me why these men are so heavily armed then? They've got enough weapons and ammo here to take on a small division.'

'See, that's the thing. These men were out to take that there herd down the water into Mexican territory. Those are top grade steers, would fetch a pretty penny for the Valquez coffers. Trouble is, where they're going there's plenty of rustlers only too willing to fight it out with a few *vaqueros* for a prize worth the taking. They have to run the gamut when they're going to the stockyards. Course he's going to protect his investment.'

'I suppose so, but there's a lot more money to be made on this side of the border. You would think he would take them to market in that direction.'

'What you just said? That's a big fat no. He'd rather make less money in one market than attract the attentions of the authorities on this side of the border.' Kent looked soberly at the body lying there. 'I'd like to shake the hand of the man who did this.'

Clayton passed a weary hand across his face but he didn't have to say anything. Blaze had replaced his patch by now but his gaze was still enough to rake through the other man.

'Can't rightly say what happened here, but I feel pretty sure our man was involved. Reckon he's a lot more dangerous than I thought.' He looked around at the scene. 'Cut right in and got them from between the trees before they could lift a single one of their weapons.' He looked down at Fernandez. 'This sure is going to make life a lot worse for us. I knew old Greedyguts was going to try and double-cross us anyway, but this means he'll be gunning for us along with the settlers.'

'Sure looks bad for us,' agreed Kent.

'Reckon we should ride like we've been set on fire and need a river to put us out,' said Blaze. 'We take as many of those guns and ammunition as we can carry and we come back for the rest.' Kent nodded his agreement. He spat on the corpse. 'Glad you're dead, you bastard. Just wish you had suffered a lot more before you got your just desserts. As for what you're saying, Thorne, I'd already decided to take their weapons when I saw this had happened.'

'We obviously had the same idea then,' said Blaze.

'What was that?' asked Clayton, looking at the two men in turn.

'We get ready for the biggest fight of our lives,' reported the farmer. 'I was once a soldier; with the help of my compatriots I think I can make a stand.'

'No use waiting around here and yakking about what we're going to do like a bunch of old women,' said Blaze.

He and Clayton helped Kent to load up the biggest and best horse that had been left stranded by the death of its owner. It had probably belonged to Fernandez. He loaded up another two and strung as many horses together as he could.

'We will have to go now,' said Blaze, 'and prepare for war.'

'What about Alice?'

'Alice,' said Blaze, 'will have to wait.'

Valquez was not a stupid man. He had regular shipments of his cattle taken down the river along with his men. When this did not happen he grew restive. He knew that they were supposed to be there by at least midday and nothing had yet happened. This time he was going to investigate for himself. It had occurred to him years before that he should get some sort of telegraph system for Hidden Valley, in order to have messages passed quickly to his home, the central point of all his operations, but he had several reasons for not doing so. One was that he had never really needed to know how well his operations were going because this was the first time they had gone awry, with non-delivery of the cattle.

He had experienced delays before which would have made such a system handy. But the biggest factor in not allowing the installation was the presence of strangers in his home territory. Valquez knew that once the strangers went away – he could hardly kill a bunch of engineers – no matter how well paid they were, rumours would soon abound about a beautiful place ruled over by a despot who paid no taxes to the Federal government. Then the real investigations would begin, and he was not even a naturalized citizen. He could very well lose everything.

So he had to put on his black jacket, long boots and dark green, wide-brimmed hat with a feather in it, the one that he thought made him look fashionable, and went down the valley to investigate what had happened. This diversion also meant that he had to cancel his daily hunting trip, another reason for feeling irritated. He took with him the six men who had come back to the fort with Blaze and Clayton. He was not in a hurry because there could have been all sorts of reasons for the delay, such as finding that some of the cattle were infected with an illness, or the men themselves falling sick. He did not really care about such things; he just wanted to know why they had not contacted him. They would be punished for this! Then his thoughts strayed to Fernandez, his mind not even daring to leap at the truth. His lieutenant seemed so solid, so commanding that he would be there until the day Don Valquez died.

For weapons he carried a Winchester rifle, a pistol in a silver holster strapped to his belt, and a sword sheathed at his side.

They rode down the natural slope leading to the

woodland that spread across the lower part of the valley and found the cattle there, with not a thing wrong with them, but no sign of his men.

'Where can they be?' he asked Pepe.

The subordinate knew better than to say that he did not know. He also knew better than to say that the men might have rebelled and gone away. Valquez did not like rebellion; those who went against his wishes usually ended up dead. Like the others before him, the woodlands seemed a natural place to start. He knew that his men had a habit of retreating there to eat, play cards and generally put the world to rights. Together with the other six, they went to the same glade where Blaze had stood not an hour before. The Don had been in war in his youth and had killed many men with his own hands since, but the sight before him made his mouth turn into a thin, grim line.

His expression changed to one of real distress when he saw the body of Fernandez. They had known each other for a long time, and the man had been an indispensable second-in-command. Don Valquez threw his head back and looked up at the tops of the green trees around him. He gave a great roar of rage and pain. Then the mist cleared and he looked at Pepe.

'Where are their horses and weapons?'

'Gone,' said Pepe. 'I have looked, the bodies have been stripped of all ammunition, their guns and horses taken away from this place of death.' The Don gave a brief nod as he strode out to the sunlight.

'Take the bodies to their homes in our own village and restore them to their families. When that is done we will regroup and destroy those who have done this thing.'

'Who?'

'Is it not obvious? This Thorne and his companion have joined forces with the settlers and would destroy all I have worked for. They have made the first act of aggression, but that has been their big mistake.'

'Why, my leader?'

'Because they will die, all of them, men, women and children, and I will have the head of Blaze on a silver platter.'

CHAPTER TEN

The three men led the string of horses out to the other side of the woods to the homestead that had been built by Kent with his own hands. You can tell a lot about a man by the condition of his home, and what Clayton and Thorne saw was a well-constructed little farmhouse made out of local wood and stone, with a large chimney at the front painstakingly created from home-made bricks cleverly augmented by stones from the riverbed. The entire building probably contained only three rooms but was so well built it could last, with care, for a century. There was a large barn that had been clearly created with the help of the entire community, when they were still talking to him, and a few little outhouses for the pigs and chickens. The farm was surrounded by neat little fields in which grew a variety of crops including corn and potatoes.

Thorne gave a few commands. He had been in a war situation before and he knew that planning was of the essence.

'Get those horses into the barn,' he said, 'or as many

as you can. Get the entire farming community together if you're able to do so, and give them the news. I want you to impress on them that they have to fight this enemy or they will die.'

'How can he do that?' asked Clayton. 'The community is spread out, so he'll never rally them in time.'

'I have a way,' said Kent grimly. As the three of them were putting the horses out of sight, three young people between the ages of ten and fourteen years old came running out to meet their father. They were followed by a woman who had a strained expression that made her look much older than her years. Kent said nothing but went over to his wife and wrapped his arms around her and held her tight.

'I thought you had gone and done something stupid,' she said.

'I didn't need to, someone did it for me,' he said, his face grim. He looked over towards the two men who were still mounted on their steeds. 'Sorry, meant to say, this is my wife Jane, my two boys John Junior and Marty, and my daughter Lynne.' Surrounded by his family, he would have looked like any other pioneer dirt farmer if it had not been for that trace of fanaticism on his face. 'Jane, this is Jubal Thorne and his friend Dan Clayton, they're going to help us.'

'We'll have to,' said Clayton in a resigned tone. 'Ain't that the case, Blaze?'

But his companion did not answer. The tall, raw-boned man had turned the colour of ivory. He closed his one good eye, gave a sigh very much like a man settling down for a long sleep, and then slid off his horse to the ground. The big quarter-horse hardly moved as this happened because he was used to unexpected events occurring around him. He probably thought this was just more of the same.

Jane came forward as Clayton slid from his own mount and she examined the man lying on the ground.

'Why, this man has been strapped up with bandages, he's had a serious wound in his side.' She put her hand down and it came back wet with blood. 'It looks as if his wound has opened up again. He needs help right now. John, Clayton, don't just stand there, help him into the house.'

'You don't have time to help him,' said her husband.

'What do you mean?'

'All of you have to get away from here right now. You remember that hunting shelter I built up in the hills amongst the trees? You have to go there, all of you, right away.'

'Why?'

'Because someone has taken the tiger by the tail and I don't want my family around when he starts biting.'

'Very well, if we must, that's what we'll do, but I still say we have to help this man.'

Knowing his wife as he did, Kent decided not to argue. He helped bring Thorne inside, ably assisted by the sheriff. Thorne's breathing was shallow and he had beads of perspiration on his forehead. This argued that he was even more ill than might have been thought, just from his wound alone. Jane got Clayton to help pull his coat off and his shirt, then she inspected the wound.

'I can sew this up,' she said, and Clayton realized he was dealing with the practical kind of pioneer woman who would do what had to be done to fix up her new guest.

'Look, I've got to rally the rest of the colony,' said Kent to Clayton and his wife. 'As soon as you get Thorne sorted out, get away from here and take what you can when you go into the hills.' Like many men, he knew there was no point in having an argument with a woman if her mind was set on getting something done. 'You, children, get everything together that you can. Get out of here as soon as possible.' The children all nodded solemnly. They were practical too. You had to be in a place like this. Their father started to leave.

'Will I come with you?' asked Clayton.

'No, the sight of a stranger might cause hostility.'

Kent departed.

Clayton shook his head as Jane began to clean up the wounded man, who they had laid out on the kitchen table. It was clear that Thorne had been concealing the wound for some time, even though it was causing him a lot of pain. He had been keeping his affliction from the other two since the time they had been up to the cabin. When Blaze learned that he was coming to the homestead he must have calculated that he would have enough time to get his task done before seeking medical attention. Unfortunately he had been wrong. He lay there now, his breathing so shallow that at times it seemed to have left his body. Clayton feared that his friend was going to die even before the war had started.

Kent knew how little time they had before Valquez would seek revenge. He rode quickly down to the village and went straight into the hall he had built there with the rest of the farmers on their arrival. Although it was not a proper church, it was where they held their Sunday service, and even had a vestigial bell tower that projected just a couple of feet above the roof. This was no mere decoration, nor was it used only on a Sunday. The settlers were far enough apart on their respective farms that the bell was used to gather them together for important meetings. Kent felt a grim smile play about his lips as he grasped the white, triple intertwined bell rope that hung down at the back of the hall. It had been his idea to bring the bell with them on their long, rocky trip. Many a voice had been raised against bringing something that did not seem to have a practical purpose. Now it was the very thing that might save their lives.

Along with his fellow colonists, he had worked out a series of chimes for different circumstances. Now he pulled on the rope six times, paused and pulled six times more. Within minutes, those from the town and their families began to pour into the tiny hamlet.

Some of them took twenty minutes or more to arrive, but he was patient, biding his time.

He had them gather in the hall and they filled it with their bodies, men, women and children, most of whom had been out working in the fields when they were called. They were rugged, simple people and now he was about to tell them that they were going to war.

'My people, I have to tell you. Today I was so desperate to end this tyranny that I went with a rifle to kill Valquez and his son.' There was a stir in the hall at this.

'Why would you do such a foolish thing?' said Ivan Goresky, the Russian émigré. 'In my country they do this, it is never the good solution.'

'He's right,' said Dorrans, 'if you have brought us here because of this, what you have done, you will bring a terrible price on our heads.'

'I didn't do it.' Kent passed a weary hand across his face. 'I realized it wouldn't be right. Not for my wife, my children or any of us.'

'Where is your family?' asked Pete Welles, a burly farmer.

'I have asked them to go to one of the hunting shelters in the hills. That is not the point, listen to me.'

'If you have killed the leader and his son you'll bring all sorts of hell down on us,' said Dorrans. 'Fernandez will ride in here with his men and attack and kill us all.'

'Will you listen to me? Fernandez won't be coming here because he's dead.'

'You killed him, too?'

'No, I didn't kill him at all.'

'But you just said he was dead.' Dorrans flung out a bony hand and addressed the entire hall, while Kent feared he might have made a mistake going there on his own. 'This man is a lunatic. I have no doubt he is telling the truth when he said he was going out to kill, for he is quite capable of doing such a thing. From what he has said in his own words, I think he has killed the leader and that Fernandez will be here.'

There was a general hubbub in the hall made louder by being in an enclosed space. Kent sensibly waited for the noise to die down, but stood his ground because he knew now that at the slightest sign of weakness, his former neighbours would be on him, only to strike him down.

'You're not listening. Any of you,' he said, his voice suddenly calm. 'Valquez is not dead, neither is his son, but Fernandez has been murdered.'

'By you!' shouted Dorrans.

'No, not by me. Let me explain what happened.'

'I'm not listening to you anymore,' said Dorrans. 'Is anyone else going to come with me?' Some people wanted to stay and hear Kent out, but it was evident that many members of the farming families were going to leave with Dorrans.

Then there was a crash as the doors of the hall were flung wide and banged into the walls on either side. The sun was still high in the sky, while the hall was lit by only a narrow window on either side, glass being at a premium in a place like this, so the light flooded through, illuminating a figure dressed in black who stood there, wearing a dark red shirt beneath his black coat, his head bare, revealing his thick, coppery locks. His face was in shadow but his whole bearing was such that everyone in the hall stopped talking, while some of the younger children gasped and pressed against their mothers. One or two of the younger women screamed. The shadowy figure came forward, his locks swinging as he took firm steps into the building.

Another man came into the hall but he was so commonplace that the eyes of the crowd barely took in his presence. Clayton stood at the back and watched.

The people parted for the demon like the red sea as he made his way to the lectern and stood there. What they saw of the ruined side of his face as his hair swung back in place did nothing to reassure them, but the silence remained.

'Ladies and gentlemen,' he said, 'and children too, I have a message for your community. My name is Jubal Thorne. Today I stopped John Kent from making a foolish decision. Along with Mr Kent, who was coming back home, I discovered that eight heavily armed *vaqueros* had been murdered while going about their business, including Fernandez. Mr Kent was not involved; I have a witness to this. Besides, who amongst you has the power to kill eight heavily armed men?'

'No,' screamed one of the women. 'What about my children?'

'The fact is, this is not a situation you wanted to be in but it is one that has occurred,' said Blaze, ignoring the interruption. 'I know who the murderer was because I was tracking the man to this valley. He will be dealt with. In the meantime the truth is simple, you have to bear arms or die because Valquez will attack. Make no bones about it.'

'He's right,' said Kent, his face now bloodless. 'You have to believe him.'

'But what can we do?' said Ivan Goresky. 'We are not heavily armed. Amongst the whole colony we have a few shotguns, some handguns and little left of ammunition; how can we fight or even defend ourselves from attacks?'

'We have brought the arms with us,' said Blaze. 'These are the arms from the men who were going to take the cattle away from here and needed to defend against marauders. Those arms are going to swing the tide in your favour. Mr Kent here has the horses and the weapons we brought with us back at his farm. Now prepare, all the women and children get into the hills where I know your men have built hunting shelters. The men come with me and we will arm you against the tyrant.'

'All this is true,' said Clayton from the front of the hall. 'I am Sheriff Clayton, I am the witness.' The colonists all turned and looked at him. There was something so real and honest about the man that they immediately believed every word.

Except for Dorrans.

'I'm not listening to any of this,' he said. 'Oh, I've no doubt you are telling the truth about the dead *vaqueros*, but I don't think Valquez will invade if he too knows the truth. He has never been attacked by our community, why would we start now?'

Dorrans stood there, tall and emaciated like one of the scarecrows that kept the rooks away from his crops.

'Valquez is a businessman, he will understand once the matter is explained to him.'

'He will understand nothing,' said Kent. 'We all know him of old, he will not stand for this and he will be completely ruthless with this community.'

There was a gleam in Dorrans's eyes that showed he could be as big a fanatic as Kent.

'Who will stand by and let this community be cut down when, by negotiating, we could save all our lives?'

Nobody responded to his words; now that the time had come for an attack, they were behind Kent and the strange new arrival with the ruined face.

They wasted no more time in discussing the matter

because most of them knew that time would pass quickly when they were preparing for any attack that would come from further up the valley. They were lucky in two respects. Most of them were ready and able to get the goods together that they needed and flee at the first sign of trouble. The second was that they knew the lie of the land, land was their business and most of them augmented their farming by hunting and shooting in the hills. They had built handy shelters up there, some being proper cabins with furniture they had made with their own hands, and a handy retreat away from the depredations of Valquez and his crew.

As they moved out of the hall, led by Kent, Blaze stood and watched them go without any expression, then when he could no longer be observed he staggered over to one of the vacant pews made from rough elm planks and sat down. He stayed that way for a few minutes, breathing deeply. Clayton arrived and sat down at his side.

'Blaze, you're sick, you shouldn't have come here.'

Just a little while earlier Clayton had witnessed an extraordinary event. Blaze had opened his eye while Jane was sewing up his wound with catgut thread. She had cleaned it with alcohol – of which they had a plentiful supply because they made it themselves – and he had said mildly:

'That sure smarts a bit.' He lay there until she was finished then he sat up, his torso bare, right there on the kitchen table and plunked his feet down on the floor. Jane had already fetched him a dark red shirt that belonged to her husband, and helped him ease it on over his bruised ribs and over the dressing that covered the stitches stretching for inches down his side.

'The children have been getting the horses ready, we can get you on the cart and out of here,' she told him. Clayton had helped him outside because the man was walking as if his whole body had slowed in time, but once he hit the fresh air he seemed to revive and shook his head.

'Now,' said Blaze, 'you get out of here with them young 'uns of yours and let me deal with the other matter.'

'I can't leave you,' she said, 'your wound will need tending.'

'I'd feel a lot better if you just went.' That was when she had departed with the children and Blaze had gone to the village to help out Kent.

'They mustn't see me like this,' he said to Clayton, 'or they'll take it as a sign of weakness. He held back and gathered his strength a little longer. 'Right, I'm ready to leave.' He got up and walked to the outside of the building. Already the men were dispersing their womenfolk and children, sending them to the hills as promised. Blaze watched them go as if he was supervising the whole event, then he got up on his horse, only a slight grimace revealing the pain that he was in.

'You're going to need rest, and soon,' said Clayton, concern showing on his kindly features.

'There'll be time enough for resting when this is all over,' said Blaze. He rode after the men as they went to Kent's farm, knowing that they would not be disappointed with what they found there. Even though the settlement consisted of only fifteen families, some of the sons were old enough to be considered men if they were over fourteen, so Kent now had about thirty male followers. He did not appear to be at all bothered that his fortunes had changed so quickly and they now accepted him as some sort of leader. They might have been farmers who worked the land just to live, but that did not mean that they were entirely unconnected with the use of guns and rifles. Between them, the eight *vaqueros* had sixteen hand guns and rifles along with plentiful supplies of ammunition. This was not including chains, daggers and clubs, all of which the farmers also possessed. In this way it was not long before everyone present had some sort of weapon, including James Dorrans, a young man of sixteen summers.

'Why are you willing to fight when your father isn't?' asked Kent, on giving the young man a club and a dagger, the guns being the preserve of the older men.

'Because I've seen the way they look at us,' said Dorrans Junior. 'It's as if they have nothing but contempt for us. We are just there to help them with their cause. Not anymore.'

By this time Blaze was at the barn with Kent, watching the weapons being handed out and guiding the farmer as to who should get what in his usual quiet manner.

'Where is his father?' he asked as the men all inspected their weapons with critical eyes. These artisans, used to working on the land, had an eye for a good tool and this was exactly what a gun or rifle was. They were soon ready for action and it seemed they were just awaiting orders, most of which they seemed to want from Blaze.

'I don't know,' answered the younger Dorrans, who had just joined the group after they had received their weapons. The worry over his missing parent was etched upon his youthful features.

Blaze stood beside his horse and directed them in easy tones. He knew that they were going to obey him because they knew he was experienced, but he had no guarantees about their survival, which was why he had asked them to send away their women and children. Most of those farmers had never fired a weapon in anger; wearily he drilled them in what they had to do.

If they lost the forthcoming battle, the leader would hunt down their loved ones in the hills and destroy them too. The stakes were high.

What worried him was the missing man.

Dorrans had last been seen riding away from the hall towards the woodlands, the gleam of fanaticism still in his eyes. Blaze hoped, with the best of motives, that the horse would stumble, throwing off the man who might cause more trouble than he was worth.

CHAPTER ELEVEN

It was getting towards night now. At this time of year, going towards autumn, it got dark fairly early in the evening even though the weather was still warm. The valley was more sheltered than the area of desert outside, which meant that it cooled down more quickly at this time when the grassy plains and the leaves of the trees absorbed the heat of the day. Dorrans felt the cooler air but knew if he made good time he could get to see the leader just before dark. He skirted around the woodlands by going through a narrow trail and found himself riding up the side of the valley that would eventually take him to the big hacienda that was really a fort.

He had not told the others, or indeed even the members of his family, that for the two years they had been the subjects of Don Valquez, he, Dorrans, had been the eyes and ears of the so-called Commander of their community. He had been paid back in several ways. His crops were left for his own use, he had been given an unlimited supply of alcohol, and he had been promised that as the community grew, he would eventually become the mayor of what might be a bustling little town. Valquez had never had any intention of letting more settlers come in, but he fed Dorrans this nonsense until the would-be-leader believed every word. Dorrans was fuelled in this by his increasing attachment to alcohol and his own sense of self-importance, which knew no bounds.

He knew that he did not have much time because this Thorne, who seemed like an experienced man, seemed to be preparing the community well for the battle to come. If Dorrans could stop that battle from happening, the community would hand over this Thorne and his companion to the true leader and their lives could continue as before.

He was met by a group of four horsemen who were riding down the plains in the opposite direction. They were led by Pepe, who had now taken over the post once held by Fernandez. They were clad in thick woollen jackets over their normal coats, because these *vaqueros* were used to being out in a variety of conditions all year round and knew how to protect their bodies. They saw Dorrans in his farming clothes and knew immediately what he was doing, just by his presence.

'Are you going to tear up the village?' asked Dorrans, as they halted and gathered around him.

'No, we have been sent as scouts,' said Pepe, 'to find out the truth of what has gone before.' He was not being entirely frank with Dorrans. Valquez was no fool. His men were not seasoned soldiers, and eight of them were gone. He wanted to find out the strength of the opposition. Good planning had been known to beat many people in an attack.

'I have come to see Valquez and let him know this can be settled well.'

'That sounds like a good idea,' said Pepe. 'We need your knowledge.'

The group of men rode hard to where Valquez had set out his camp. He had a number of smaller quarters, barely visible because they were built amongst the trees. He used these as his hunting lodges if he had to stay out for the night, or when he was conducting some kind of business with his men. Outside the woodlands, on the plain, were the tents of his followers. They had gone at such a speed to get there in barely half an hour that Dorrans's horse, an old mare he used in his daily business, could barely keep up with the others, but she was game enough to keep going. The light was fading rapidly now as the evening started to come on in earnest.

Pepe led Dorrans to the door of the lodge. Valquez himself answered.

'Ah, my friend, come in.' He led Dorrans to the interior where a roaring fire burned in the grate and there was a large rocking chair beside the fireplace. On a low table sat a bottle of mescal and several glasses. 'You drink?'

After his long ride Dorrans had a thirst on him like a man in a desert. He gave a nod and received a full glass which he swallowed in seconds.

'Again?' Valquez refilled the glass and took some as well. 'So, my friend, what brings you here?'

'I want to let you know that Kent had nothing to do with those murders.'

'Is that so? Tell me more.'

'He came back to the village to let us know about the murdered *vaqueros*. He was there along with that strange hunter.'

'Blaze?'

'I don't know that name, said he was called Jubal Thorne.'

'That is his name, Blaze the bounty hunter.'

'This has been a terrible mistake. Kent would never be able to kill that many armed men.'

'But this Blaze might be able to do so?'

'I don't know anything about him,' confessed Dorrans.

'What has he done with your people?'

'He has asked them to prepare for war because he does not think you will listen to reason.'

'How heavily armed are your people?'

'I don't know.' Dorrans suddenly realized that he should have waited to see the strength of armaments held by the man. 'He was using weapons he had gained from the dead men.'

'What about your own weapons, I mean, those owned by the settlers?'

'We have very few, some rifles and handguns and very little ammunition.'

'But those *vaqueros* were heavily armed for their journey,' said Valquez. 'Still, they did not have enough weapons to arm thirty men. Is all of what you have told me true?'

'I swear to God.'

'Here is the Bible,' said Valquez. It was the one book he had in all of his homes. 'Lay your hand on it now and swear again.'

'I swear all I have told you is true.'

'Very well.' Valquez looked at him with calculating eyes. 'I believe this Kent had nothing to do with the killings, but I see that dog Thorne is using you. This must have been his deed.'

'Send me back and I will get the people on my side. I will send him to you.'

'My friend, I will send you back to the village all right. Come with me.' He led his visitor outside. The air was fresh and cold. Valquez took out the silver handled pistol he always kept at his side. He pointed it at Dorrans and shot him in the heart at point-blank range. The man gave a low moan and crumpled to the ground.

'Pepe,' said Valquez, 'Get this on his horse and lead it to the forest trail, the beast will find its own way after that.'

'Yes, Commander.' Pepe did not relish the idea of riding out as it was getting dark, but he could steer well enough by the light of the stars.

'And Pepe.'

'Yes, Commander?'

'We attack at dawn.'

Blaze had not told his companions, but he had been there when a town had been attacked before, and he knew what it was like to watch women and children die. They had decided that they would set up brushwood around the village as a natural barrier in case the men came during the night, then they had taken their shovels and dug defence pits all around the area. It was Blaze who had asked them to do this. A man attacking with a gun from such a pit would have a good place to hide before launching his attack. The preparation was good for the men because it kept them busy at a critical time when they might have been worrying about their loved ones.

After he had instructed the men, Thorne had personally gone to supervise the departure of the women to the hills. They were not entirely unarmed either because one or two had shotguns and they had plenty of knives. By separating into their respective hiding places they would be harder to track down, since it would be far easier to destroy them if they were all sheltering in one place.

Clayton was at his side in all of this.

'I'm worried about you,' he said. 'You don't look well.'

'I'm all right,' said Blaze grimly. 'I have to be until nightfall.'

'Why nightfall?'

'Because our enemy, if he has any sense, will wait until daylight before he attacks. Remember, even professional soldiers don't like to attack at night and these men are not a trained army.'

At this point they had seen the last of the families get into the hills. The day was by no means over for the women and children, but at least they were all safely out of sight. Valquez had neither the time nor the resources to hunt down the rest of the families and fight their men folk at the same time.

Thorne rode back down to the village and inspected the new fortifications with interest. These were able men who had constructed well in a short time.

The village was a short ride from the woodland that made a natural break across the valley. It was now so dark that one or two lamps had been lit to allow the job to be completed. The tree line was just one undistinguished mass in front of them, but as they stood there – the men who were finishing off their fortifications, Thorne and Clayton – a dark object came away from the mass and moved towards them.

Blaze instantly had his guns in his hand. If it was a lone gunman he would soon regret trying to tangle with them.

Instead, as the object came closer, he saw it was a big mare, but instead of a rider in the traditional position, there was a form lying slumped across the saddle.

Dorrans's son, Jim, flung down the shovel he had been holding and ran across to the horse with a cry of pure distress on his lips.

'Father! Dad, what have they done?' He grabbed his father's legs and the man slid to the ground and sprawled on his back. They did not even need the gaping wound in his chest to see that he was stone dead.

'I think they've sent us a message,' said Blaze.

The boy looked at his dead father, tears running down his face.

'I will avenge your death,' he said. He looked around at the older men around him and added, 'Help me bury my father.'

Blaze did not have to say anything as the man was laid to rest. What they had seen was an object lesson in the man who was going to lead battle against them. The men knew now that they were not making all these preparations just on a whim, that they were in real danger, and as the night came on them they were bedded down and ready for the fight of their lives.

No one would sleep well that night.

Up in the hills, Alice looked down on the lights of encampment down below and shivered. She was high up in the heights along with Shannon. Since the murder of the *vaqueros* he had said very little to her. Her head was filled with questions but she dreaded asking him anything now, too frightened of his reaction.

They were in a cavern that had been scooped out on the side of the hill by combined natural erosion from wind and water. As a shelter, it was barely big enough for the two of them, and it contained as many goods as they had been able to carry along with the canvas bag in which resided a fortune. They had plenty of bedding and were warm enough, but she kept as far away from him as possible in a limited space. The situation was made worse by the fact that they dared not light a lamp or candle. She now hated and dreaded him more than any other person she had known.

The strange thing was that since they had moved here, he had been thoughtful and kind towards her, making sure that she was well fed (although she just picked at her food) and had enough to drink. He even tried to give her as much privacy as he could in a limited space. He had been a perfect gentleman too. When he brought her here, she feared what he was going to do to her, but he had left her alone and even showed concern for the bruising on her face that he had put there.

Yes, for the time being he was the gentle, kind and amusing River she had known back in her home town, but for some reason this scared her as much as his violent outbursts.

'What's going on down there, do you think?' he asked quietly, his voice concealed from below by the brisk soughing of the wind through the trees and the rustling of leaves.

'I think that some people who live in the valley are being picked on,' said Alice without any colour in her voice, 'and I think it's because of those dead *vaqueros*.'

'Oh that.' Shannon gave a light laugh as if they were talking about an embarrassing accident. 'Well, that's up to them, isn't it?'

'You started it.' She felt nothing but fear, hatred and loathing for him now.

'Must admit, it's put a cramp on my plans. I was going to lie low here for a month then sneak us off to the nearest town and get us hitched.'

'I don't—'

'You don't what?' He searched her face in the fading light. She shrank away from him in the little space she had.

'I don't know if it will be that easy,' she said.

'Getting out of here? Not a problem. We'll wait until this is all over, then we'll sneak out of the valley with as many supplies as we can take, make our way to Hixby, get some more food and water, and go into Colorado. Once there we can do what we need to do. It's just a pity.' Shannon looked at the flickering lights below.

'What's a pity?'

'Shame I'm going to miss a good fight. I'd love to see

what happens, but that's life, you can't have everything. I'm happy as long as I have you.' He embraced the girl tenderly. 'You're cold, come inside and warm up, we'll be fine.' He waited until she was back inside the cave and followed her inside. In here, he risked lighting a candle for a short while so they could see what they were doing.

Alice sat wrapped against the cold in her blankets, pretending after a while to go to sleep. Once Shannon fell asleep she was out of here. She didn't care anymore.

CHAPTER TWELVE

Blaze rested through the night in one of the four houses in the village. This belonged to an elderly woman, Mrs Welles, the mother of one of the farmers, but they had made him up a comfortable bed in the front room. This was in deference to the wound in his side. He ate well and drank copious amounts of whatever liquids he could get hold of, and fell asleep quickly, just as if he had nothing on his mind. Not letting things that had not happened trouble him was an art he had learned long ago. Clayton, who sat in a chair alongside his new friend, wished that he had the same attitude. He had elected to stay on watch because he knew that he was not going to sleep, and kept his Winchester rifle loaded and by his side at all times. Blaze got up early and went off to do something by himself, but Clayton was asleep in the chair by then.

In the meantime the hall next door had been turned into a minor fort, where the men had all assembled. They slept on the floor on bedrolls. Patrols had been established to go around the perimeter of their new fortifications and the men were relieved every two hours so that when the attack came, everyone would have had some sleep.

These were men fighting now for something they believed in. A lot of them cursed Kent and Blaze for dragging them into this mess, but at the same time many of them were relieved that they were going to take a stance against the man who had taken everything that was rightfully theirs, leaving them only the barest resources. What could have turned into a bustling town with more movement of settlers from outside had been halted by the actions of Valquez and his determination to hold on to land which was not even his.

Just before dawn, the men were all up and ready to take their positions. Many of them were yawning and bleary-eyed, having been awake most of the night through worry. Some were even doubtful about an attack taking place at all.

'It's real quiet, nobody's heard a thing,' said Welles to Kent as they stood outside the hall. 'Are you sure this is gonna happen?'

'If I hear that kind of talk again,' said Kent, who was now their war leader, 'I'm going to have you locked up for the duration. A man who doesn't believe in what's going to happen is a danger to himself and others. Don't you go around spreading doubt, that's the last thing we need.'

The men were shadowy figures around the area. Blaze came out of the house in which he had been sleeping, his black coat flapping in the morning breeze, his Stetson tilted at an angle. Horses had been saddled and were waiting at the back of the hall. This wasn't just going to be a ground battle. The armed troops were already in position in their dugouts. He said little to the men standing there as he came forward, Clayton with him. They got ready to get into the saddle at the last moment.

The gunfighter seemed to be moving more slowly than ever before. Clayton was worried about him, and although he did not like to admit the fact to himself, he was also doubtful about Blaze's ability to carry out his plans for the coming battle. He could not say why, but he had a feeling that Thorne's presence was crucial in the up and coming fight.

'Are you OK?' asked Clayton. 'You shouldn't even be fighting in your state.'

'I'll be fine,' was the laconic reply. 'Wound stiffened up a bit during the night is all.'

As the men waited beside their mounts, those who were manning the dug-outs stole out in the semi-darkness and took up their positions. The holes in the ground – ten in all – had been spaced widely apart and dug between the woodlands and the village. As the men climbed in to wait, Jim and the other lads from the community concealed their presence by laying hastily woven mats of grass and twigs over the top of their places of concealment. Although made quickly and of rough materials, the mats were amazingly effective, their very roughness meaning that they blended in with the natural landscape.

Blaze was glad that he was not down one of those holes. He could imagine being there when the battle began. The person would hear the pounding of hoofs coming towards him, not knowing if half a ton of horseflesh was going to stumble on the edge and land on top of him.

As the light grew there was a period of time that seemed to stretch out forever. The landscape was devoid of movement. Nothing could be heard but the birdsong in the trees, the clap of rooks' wings as they rose up to hunt in the light of dawn, and the occasional sound of the horses neighing and snorting as they waited restlessly beside their grim owners in the area outside the village hall.

The sun had hardly started to rise when there was a movement in the distant line of the trees. Blaze wondered how long the enemy had been there. He hoped that they had not seen the men taking position. His hopes were bolstered by the fact that every single *vaquero* was seated on his mount. That meant that they must have walked their horses on foot through the woodland trail before assembling them in line for battle and that would have taken some amount of time, meaning that they had just taken up position.

Someone on Valquez's side blew a battle horn, and then the charge began, led by the old war-horse himself.

Valquez was dressed in black trousers with a gold stripe up the side. He wore a military-style jacket in tasteful grey and black with gold buttons holding the tunic together. They must have been well sewn on, given his corpulent frame. On his cuffs he had gold braid that set off a further line of three buttons down his sleeves, while he had wide epaulettes on his broad shoulders. His collar was high and stiff to protect his neck. On his head he wore a flat grey hat with a black shiny peak. This hat was secured under his multiple chins by a piece of black silk braid. He held the reins with one hand and a short, military sword in the other. At his side, in a saddle sheath, was a slightly more deadly rifle.

His waxed moustache bristled even more splendidly than those of his dead lieutenant. Not only was Valquez leading the charge, he was doing his task so vigorously that his men were having difficulty keeping up with him. The entire troop consisted of about forty horses. The *vaqueros* on the big, dark brown Mexican horses made a sight as they rode towards the barriers. In deference to the cold of the morning, most of them wore big woollen comforters in various shades of red, blue and green, over which they had slung their bullet belts. Unlike their leader they were waving carbines, Winchester rifles and Colt handguns, some of which looked quite old, arguing that Valquez must have had to break out the last of his armoury. The men looked as huge and menacing as their horses.

In contrast Blaze had ten horses and riders. The paucity of men under his command did not daunt him in the least. He had always believed that if a man is fearless there is nothing that can stop him from winning through. He was fearless himself for the very good reason that he felt his soul had died a long time ago and that he had nothing left to live for. At least that had been his approach to life until now.

The settlers had provided him with his greatest impetus for a long time. He knew that if this battle ended in defeat for their men folk, all the women and children sheltering in the hills would be hunted down and mercilessly slaugh-tered like so many helpless rabbits. He was a far from sentimental man – the life he led had knocked all of that nonsense out of him – but when he thought of those good women who had given up so much to be here, and all of those tender lives yet unrealized, his blood, what was left of it, reached boiling point.

As soon as he saw the formation coming forward from the tree line, he got up onto his horse a little stiffly. If only Kent and the rest had known the effort this took. He turned and looked at the men waiting expectantly behind him, gave a satisfied nod and pulled his thick, coppery hair back from the ruined side of his face and pulled up the fleshy eye patch to reveal the skeletal orbit and the staring eye within. One or two of the men gave him a startled look, and one even crossed himself.

As Valquez and his men pounded across the plain towards them Blaze pointed forward and shouted, 'Charge!'

The rough wooden barriers at the front of the village had been pulled back by some of the boys so that the horsemen could stream through, then the barriers were pulled back across again.

The rebel settlers were determined that Valquez was not going to take that which had taken them so long to build.

Four to one? The *vaqueros* were grinning in anticipation of the rout that was to follow. Along with their glorious leader they would decimate these ten puny horsemen, take the village and kill the rest at their leisure.

Only Valquez seemed a little disappointed at this poor show. He was a hunter and would have liked a better fight.

He was to get a better fight than he could have anticipated. As Blaze gave his opening roar, the men who had hidden earlier threw aside their grassy coverings and crawled out to the plain. The roar had been their signal to emerge. Not all of them were armed with guns or rifles because of the limited number of those weapons available. Five of them had long clubs or metal farming implements and were interspersed between those who had handguns or rifles. As they emerged they all roared and shouted in unison to attract the attention of the marauders.

This meant that instead of riding down ten horsemen, the *vaqueros* now had people behind them too. Their forty horses could easily have ridden down the ten, but now they were fighting a battle on two levels. Best of all, from the viewpoint of the village, the men on the ground did not waste any time. Those with guns and rifles began to fire on the horsemen at the rear. Even better, from their point of view, those with clubs ran forward and knocked their weapons into the hind legs of the horses, hitting them good solid blows. It was a thing they did with regret because the horse is the farmer's friend, but in this case there was nothing else they could do. Six horses fell or reared up according to their injuries, unseating their riders, most of whom fell heavily to the ground. Those men who fell were immediately set upon and most did not rise again.

Valquez was, of course, furious.

'Ride forward,' he shouted.

But the horsemen were now split between trying to get the enemy from behind and dealing with those who were shooting from the front. Instead of an orderly line the ten village horsemen were now in a milling, stamping group of men and horses, shooting into them at will. Valquez slashed out with his sword, stabbing into one of the villagers, who fell from his horse with a scream of pain, his arm half-severed.

Blaze took aim as coolly as if he was sitting beside the fire at home and shot at the sword hand. There was a loud ping! as the bullet hit the metal and the shock drove up the arm of the leader. He gave a shouted curse and dropped the weapon to the ground. Seeing this, Blaze rode hard towards him. He was solely focused on getting to the leader and oblivious to the other men around him.

Valquez was struggling to draw his rifle from its sheath. His saddle was so big and comfortable it was really a kind of shield, but the height of the sides made it hard for him to release the weapon. This was when he looked up and saw the gunman heading towards him. He had never seen an enemy like this in his life. With his dark copper hair streaming out behind him as he rode, and that skeletal aspect to his face, Blaze looked like some demon released from hell. For the first time in his life, Valquez turned and rode away from the scene of a fight. He was just trying to get some breathing space to get out his weapon, but it looked like cowardice and some of his men, seeing this, also broke away from the fight and began to flee.

Blaze caught up with the man, but instead of shooting him point blank as he could have done, he used his powerful right fist to punch Valquez on the side of his head, then he grabbed a fistful of the military-style tunic. The horse continued onwards, but Valquez was swept out of the saddle and fell heavily to the ground. They had landed just short of one of the dug-outs. Blaze wasted no time but dragged Valquez into the hideout. In the general confusion no-one but Clayton, who was following Blaze closely, had seen what had happened. It looked as if their leader had disappeared off the face of the earth.

To say that the *vaqueros* were frightened would be an understatement. Blaze had covered their leader with one of the grassy mats, and now stood with his pistols at the ready waiting to shoot anyone who dared to come near him. They did not know he was concealing Valquez, to him he looked like a frightening, capable enemy.

An additional factor was the presence of Kent, who turned out to be an excellent shot. He had two kills to his name already, wounding another three men.

Pepe gave a shrill command for the men to retreat. They looked for their leader but saw only his horse running across the plain. These men were not professional fighters; now that they knew their enemy had teeth they were more than ready to depart the field of battle. As if they were one entity they turned and rode back towards the woodlands. Blaze found a husky boy standing beside him, while Clayton sat close, still on his horse.

'Jim,' said Blaze. 'Help me right now.'

They went into the dug-out. Blaze and the young man swiftly stripped off the fancy hat and jacket. Valquez was groaning and semi-conscious.

'Clayton, you wait here and cover us,' said Blaze. 'Come on, Jim, we've got to lift this fat bastard and get him to the village.' Together the two picked up the man who had caused so much trouble. They were partly concealed by Clayton, who put his horse between the dug-out and the woods. Even so they had a fairly wide stretch of open ground to cover.

Only Pepe, who seemed to be looking out for his Commander, noticed what they were doing. To the rest of the fleeing *vaqueros* it seemed as if the two were just trying to rescue a wounded man.

'Open the barriers,' screamed Blaze, using what little breath he had to spare. His side was aching abominably even though they had covered about half the distance. It didn't help that they had to dodge riderless horses and dead bodies on the way.

Pepe shouted a swift command and two of his men came to his side, wearing looks of fear.

'See, he has taken our leader,' he said in Spanish. 'We must get him at all costs.'

The three riders thundered in a direct line towards their target. If they were timely they could cut down young Jim and Blaze to get their leader back. Abruptly they were blocked by Clayton, who rode across their path. Clayton was no mean shot. He fired and the man to the left of Pepe gave a scream of pain and fell off his steed. Clayton fired again, the bullet missing Pepe by a scant inch. The *vaquero* knew that Clayton was being stubborn, that he would never let them pass to get to their fallen leader and rescue him, so he raised his gun and shot Clayton in the chest at point-blank range. Clayton tightened his finger on the trigger for one last time and the shot caught his assassin on the upper arm, but just nicking the surface through the thick clothing the man wore, causing him to wince in pain.

Clayton died in the saddle, slumping forward without falling off, his feet firmly in the stirrups, those devices keeping him in place. His horse turned and ran to the nearest place of safety, knowing that something had gone badly wrong with its master, and that place was the village. As it ran, Blaze and his helper managed to reach the barriers. These were shoved apart enough to let them through with their load. They dropped Valquez just inside. Then Blaze was faced by the corpse of his friend riding through the still open gap. He gave a great cry of rage and took his pistols out from his deep pockets. The horseman beside Pepe, seeing the danger they were in, tried to pull up his horse but he was too late; the demon with the ruined face blasted forth, twin bursts of fire coming from his weapons in quick succession. The *vaquero* hit the soil with an almighty thud, but the deputy leader pulled away and rode off as quickly as he could. He might have been loyal to Valquez, but he was not stupid. Besides, he was terrified of the man with the demon face.

When their shelter proved to be above the rallying point for the leader and his *vaqueros*, Alice was filled with fear for their lives.

'How are we going to get away now?' she asked in barely a whisper, but River was nonchalant about their prospects.

'This here's just temporary. But just to make sure, I'm gonna load up the Winchester and ma Colts. They'll get us taken out if they come near us, girl.' He then put a reassuring hand on her arm and did not seem to notice that she shrank away from him. He took out his Winchester, then hunted for the bullets.

'Damn, looks as though I've run out of ammo for this

thing. Never mind, there's enough up the spout for a long-range kill or two, then if they get close I'll get them with these beauts.' He twirled his army Colts. Shannon was truly alive now. The girl had never seen him so animated. He truly thought that two handguns and a rifle with a few bullets in it would defeat a small army of *vaqueros*.

However, he wasn't as stupid as he seemed and kept the noise they made to the minimum by limiting their movement within the cave. This was helped by the fact that those below were noisy themselves in going about their business. Once, just as it was getting dark, they heard the sound of gunshots.

'They ain't bothered about us,' said Shannon, 'they're looking for much bigger fish.'

Nonetheless it was still a fitful night for the girl. She could not look for the mercy of those below and she was trapped with a killer who might also be a madman. Just before dawn, she was alerted to the sounds of horses moving out.

'Looks like the fight's about to start,' said Shannon, managing to peer over the edge. 'Well, once we've had some eats we'll set up watch.' He was as good as his word.

After the men were all gone, Shannon produced a length of rope which he tied around the girl's wrists, leaving a length he could trail out behind him. He took the rifle in one hand and dragged her behind him with the other. He was surprisingly strong for one of his build. They came to an area above and to the side of the lodge where the plains could be seen between the trees.

There was a fallen tree that lay on its side just at that

point, jammed in such a way that it made an ideal resting place for someone keeping watch. He wasted no time, lashing the other end of the rope to a branch, but in such a fashion that the girl was able to sit higher up.

'Your job is to sit still. If you see anything I don't, warn me, but that's it,' he said. Then he moved down the hill to the fallen tree, rested the barrel of the rifle on a natural groove in the bark, jammed his hat on his head, and waited.

Above him the girl said nothing, did not even try to converse with him, but waited too. When she saw that he was concentrating all of his attention on what was happening down below, she began to work on the ropes he had tied around her wrists, using her teeth of all things to help loosen the bonds. The rope finally fell away with a slight whisper and she caught it, wrapping it lightly around her wrists so that if he looked back a cursory glance might show that she was still tied up.

In the distance the sounds of the battle had long since died down. Now, as he waited for whatever might be the sequel to that event, the girl watched him.

She was waiting for the right time to make her move.

Blaze got the boys to carry Valquez into the village hall. While they did so he gave himself the grim task of untangling Clayton's body from the reins that had kept him on the back of his horse. Almost tenderly he laid his friend beside the village hall. Clayton had been a good man. Sometimes a little slow on the uptake, but stolid and worthy, a good back up in times of trouble, and he had paid the ultimate price for his loyalty. With this eulogy ringing in his mind, Blaze made sure that the remaining men and boys were keeping guard in case of a further attack.

What followed was not that difficult in terms of what had to be done, but it was hard for both parties considering what had just happened outside. The hardest part was restraining Kent and his fellows, in persuading them that it was in their interests not to kill Valquez there and then.

When he came fully around, the old leader was bullish and defiant. The one thing that he did not lack was courage. This was a man who, from his youth, colonized this valley and made it his own. Even though he was tied up and surrounded by his enemies, he invited them to untie his bonds and give him a fair swordfight with Kent, then they would see who the better man was. Instead Blaze stood between the two men. His voice was deliberately calm.

'You will both sign a treaty that allows you to live in this valley, not as master and servants, but as landowners and workers. You both know it is the only way if you are to have peace. If not you will always be sniping at each other and no-one will be safe. This way you are both winners.' With a flourish he produced two identical scrolls of paper. 'I drew up these in the early hours of the morning.' He looked intently from one man to the other. 'You will both sign these, and then you will return to your own people and get your lives back.'

The astonished Don Valquez and John Kent both scrutinized the document. It was written in neat, not showy writing and enshrined the rights of the farmers to continue their work in peace, but also agreed to give Valquez his cattle rights and the ability to run his business without having them undermined.

As documents go it was well-written, straight to the point, but above all, it was fair.

'I know we all have the bodies of friends and comrades lying out there,' said Blaze, wincing at his own words as Clayton came to mind. 'But a treaty is the only way.'

'And if I don't sign?' asked the Don bluntly.

'Well, I can tell you, Valquez, there is a criminal loose in this valley. If I don't get him, the outside authorities will get impatient and send more men. When they find out how you have been living here without paying taxes, I'm sure the Federal government will be taking a lot more interest in you, Don Valquez. The choice is yours.'

For the former ruler, life was economic; if anything could change his mind it was those words. The old scoundrel winced at the thought of what the government would do to him if they found out he was here. His son had been born on this soil, so if the son was left the land he could claim it was his as a citizen of the country, but Valquez did not have that protection.

Worse still, if he did not agree with the authorities they could merely declare he was an illegal person and throw him out of the country, taking everything in his coffers. He looked Blaze straight in the eye.

'Where do I sign, *hombre?*'

The end was not far off after that. Two of the settlers had been killed as well as four *vaqueros*. Many more were wounded on both sides. Due to their diligence in picking up the rest of the weapons from the battlefield, the settlers were now more heavily armed than the *vaqueros*.

Don Valquez went out with an escort and brought in his new lieutenant to sit down with the farmers and beat out a more detailed settlement between them.

Kent took no pleasure in forging a treaty with Don Valquez; as far as he was concerned his people should have been free from them the moment they came to Hidden Valley. He stopped Blaze as the bounty hunter was leaving to carry out his final task.

'Don't worry about your friend Clayton, I'll see that he's buried all right.'

'OK.' Blaze showed very little emotion at this at first, and then he gave Kent one of his rare smiles. 'Make this treaty work. It's your only chance.' He left the hall and went out to where Clayton lay beside the others, his hands across his chest. His eyes were closed and he looked as if he was asleep.

'Thanks,' said Blaze, as if to no-one in particular, then strode off. He made sure his horse was properly saddled, the cinch straps tightened, and then he took out his guns and made sure they were fully loaded. He got on his horse and rode out of the village without looking back.

CHAPTER THIRTEEN

Blaze had one problem left. Now he had to track down a deadly killer and his kidnap victim. That was all right in theory, but in a valley that was over sixteen miles long, this left him a lot of room in which to work.

He did a lot of thinking.

It was obvious that Shannon had been here before. He wouldn't want to bring any attention to himself so he would keep away from the farmlands and the settlers, so that took away the bottom third of the valley. Equally he would not venture out on the plains where he could be seen by the *vaqueros*. He might have managed to kill eight of them when he was concealed by trees, but he would not take the same risk out in the open. This meant he would have taken shelter in the wooded hills to the side of the valley.

Shannon would find plenty of shelter there amidst the cedars, cottonwoods and willows that grew so abundantly in the slopes.

Satisfied inside his mind with the idea that this would be the case, he decided to rely on one last factor to help him resolve this issue. He would proceed on pure instinct alone. With this thought in mind, he took his horse over the side of the wooded area at the sloping hills and had the animal move at a walking pace, while Blaze looked upwards to see if he could spot a feature that would draw his attention. That was when he came across the hunting lodge belonging to Valquez.

Above the lodge, he noticed, was an area where the trees had been thinned out. That made sense because roots could come loose and it lessened the danger of the ledge being flattened if a tree came down in the winter rains. Above the tree line frowned the cliff that separated Hidden Valley from the outside world. This was an area that had been pock-marked by millennia of wind, rain and water erosion from streams trickling through, in the same manner that had created the Whispering Canyon which had given Blaze and Clayton access to this beautiful, deadly place. His instincts immediately began coming into force when he saw that above the lodge was an area of overhanging rock that provided shelter from the winter weather for the building below. If it could provide shelter for one person it could do so for another. He decided to tether his horse further along then come back and investigate on foot. If he was right he would find their horses tethered at the foot of the hill, concealed in woodland away from this spot, but far enough away not to arouse attention.

It was as he was riding away to investigate that the disaster happened. His instincts had been proved correct to a catastrophic degree. He had quickened his horse's pace to that of a canter, but even this was no protection from the bullet that zinged down from the hill above. Fortunately for Blaze, but not for the horse, it is difficult to time a shot well enough to hit a moving target. The bullet missed Blaze and hit his horse in the head. The animal gave a distressed whinny then keeled over as blood spurted forth, and died on the green sward. Luckily the hunter still had the ability to move at an uncanny speed when he needed to do so. He flung himself off the animal as it fell. If he was trapped beneath this amount of horseflesh he would be a sitting duck. Unfortunately he was not able to fling his body completely clear; the dying animal landed flank first on his right leg, trapping that limb. A bolt of agony shifted up the extremity, but more importantly he felt the wound on his side become wet again with the force of the fall.

He lay there winded for a few seconds, but could not allow himself the luxury of staying there. The horse went into spasms as it died and during one of these it shifted sufficiently to allow him to withdraw his leg. His ankle was in agony. Even as he tried to move, another bullet zinged past his head. He was just glad that he had fallen into the edge of the woodland; this meant that the gunman in the hills could not see him properly, or that bullet would have been in his head. Although an uncanny shot, Blaze knew that if he stayed and tried to fight at that particular moment, he was going to die. With this thought in mind, he pulled away from the edge and stumbled into the thick canopy of trees that lay beyond the lodge. Branches tore at his coat and his face as he made his way in but he was soon amid the thick brushwood. His ankle screamed at him to stop but he ignored the pain and continued onwards, trying to find a spot where he could rest and keep watch at the same time for the gunman.

For what seemed like an endless time, he pushed aside the spiny branches that tore at his hair, his face and his body, until he emerged into a clearing where the ground was rockier and it was hard for the trees to get purchase on the ground. The clearing was big enough for him to get some shelter, and best of all there was another stream running down the middle, gurgling over some large red, grey and brown pebbles. A jumble of dry, even bigger stones, lay to the side of the stream.

Blaze laid out his guns, which he had kept intact in his deep pockets, on one of the large, dry rocks so that they were close at hand, then he threw off his coat, pulled off his left boot and thrust his foot into the water. Coming as it did from some underground source that trickled outwards, the water was very cold. He felt another shock go through his system but his swollen ankle responded to the treatment well and the swelling began to go down almost at once. He held it there for a few minutes before withdrawing his foot. He dried his foot on some leaves then put his boot back on before walking up and down for a few minutes. The pain and swelling had subsided. Although he still felt twinges when he walked, the sensation was much easier to deal with.

He felt a touch of regret at doing this because he was losing valuable time when the attacker would be getting away, but there was only one route, besides the river, out of this valley and Blaze knew that it was in his own ability to get another horse from the farmers just a few miles away.

Then it was time to look at his side. As he had guessed the wound had opened up again, mainly because he hadn't lain down enough to give it time to heal. Luckily though, Jane had used a lot of material when she strapped him up, and not all of his stitches had given way. He tore off some of the generous binding, used it as a washing rag to clean his side, and then bound up the wound. He had done this kind of thing for his body before.

Again this had taken him more time than he really wanted to spare, but he could not see what else he could do if he wanted to continue. Finally he lay down, cupping his hands and drank long and deep from the stream. He stood up, feeling refreshed. He was ready to go now. But what direction should he take?

The decision was made for him when he heard the screams of a young woman coming from his left. He began to move upwards, slowing down as the woodland grew thicker.

High up on the hill, Shannon peered downwards but could see nothing now except for the dead horse, which had kicked its last only a few seconds before. Although he had never seen Jubal Thorne, the man known as Blaze, before, such was the reputation of the man hunter that the minute he appeared, Shannon recognized him from the many descriptions he had heard on his travels. It is one of the truths of criminality that such people talk to each other; Shannon even recognized the thick coppery locks and long black trail coat. The trouble was that the form of the hunter was like that of a ghost because he kept disappearing in front of the trees that were left, while he kept plodding along.

Shannon had fired his shot at Blaze's body just as the gunman shifted position and walked onwards a little faster. The shot had made Blaze hasten forward causing him to stumble on the uneven ground and fall forward. He had seen the movement and tried to adjust his aim but had not succeeded in doing so. But then he saw the gift that he had been given as Blaze lay sprawled on the ground. The gunman was ready to be finished off like the sitting duck he now was. Shannon raised his rifle again – a bullet from a pistol would never have reached that distance – and tightened his finger on the trigger at the same instant as a slim foot came in from behind and hit him on his right shoulder blade; this knocked through to the barrel of the rifle. The weapon was tightly held by the gunman, so the barrel was only deflected by an inch or two, but due to the logistics of shooting, it meant that his bullet missed Blaze by a couple of feet as the trajectory of the shot widened out. This was enough for Blaze to get to his feet and vanish into the dense tangle of vegetation at the foot of the hill.

Shannon turned and saw that the girl was standing defiantly above him on the slope. There was a look on her face that he was unable to read, something between fear, bravery and defiance. She was determined to stand up to him now at any cost.

'Haven't you killed enough people already? Look at the damage you've caused to this place, you've started a civil war by killing those men when you could just have held them up and gotten me away. They just needed to be stopped is all.'

'I've killed men for less,' snarled Shannon as he swung the gun barrel in her direction.

For one heart-stopping moment it looked as though he was going to put a bullet in her heart. Then he gave the girl a lop-sided charming grin that would have fooled her only a few days before.

'Do you realize what you've done, my love? That man down there is real dangerous. He could put a cramp on all our dreams if he survives. Don't know if he will, though, I'm not sure if one of my bullets got him, what with all the blood spilling out of his shitty horse.'

Shannon had been lying against a fallen tree, which had anchored him on the steep slope that led down to the plains. This took his weight while he carried out his self-allotted task. Now he was finding it a little awkward to get back up.

'Here, hold this while I push with my feet,' he said to the girl, stretching out his arm with the rifle at the end. She seized the barrel and held the weapon with wonder written all over her face.

'Don't worry, it's not loaded now,' he grunted, 'we used up all the shots.'

Even if he loved the girl he was not stupid enough to hand her a loaded rifle. He was not unaware of the way she looked at him now. Alice held the rifle for a second as if she was about to throw it down, but as he pulled his body upwards she swung it by the barrel with great force and the wooden stock of the gun banged against the side of his head.

If the situation had not been so desperate she would have laughed at the expression on his face, because he looked like a man who had bit into a delicious steak only to find the meat was rancid. At the same time he lost his grip on the vegetation and started rolling down the steep hill. This also had the effect of putting him out of her reach so that she was unable to administer any more blows, including the knockout she desired.

She threw down the rifle and the force of the movement pulled the trigger. There was a sharp crack as a bullet came out and whistled through the undergrowth. She hastily picked up the weapon and checked it for bullets, which she should have done in the first place, but it was now empty as she verified when she clicked the trigger while pointing it at him. Obviously he had made a misjudgement and had been wrong about the rifle being empty when it was handed to her. For a second she could have wept.

Alice was not the kind of person who dwelt too much on her mistakes and in this case, she was wise not to do so. Shannon had recovered quickly enough from the blow for his expression to turn from one of distaste to murderous hatred.

'You hit me, you *bitch*,' he snarled, coming up the banking towards her, his heels breaking loose the dark soil that pattered beneath, halting his progress for a few seconds. Any delay was long enough for the girl.

She tried not to descend into blind panic, an easy enough thing to do considering that she was dealing with a deranged killer. Instead she pulled back and ran upwards. Instinctively she knew that if she went down that way he would be on to her in a second.

The valley had been formed in such a way that the rocky wall that separated it from the rest of the world on this side had a series of natural grooves in the soft stone. These grooves ran for many miles along the valley, forming a kind of natural trail. This was broken at intervals, but not so much that she would be unable to run along. Indeed it was this method that had allowed them to get to the cave in which they had sheltered for so long.

She stumbled at the very entrance to the cave. This was not a good thing for her to do, because she could hear her captor at her heels. He was panting heavily as he crashed through the undergrowth and scrabbled up the hill. Despite his habit of smoking his Bull Durham cigarettes, and heavily at that, he was young enough not to have broken his breath, so he still had enough control to speak to her. This was the worst part, because his panted words were in the form of a plea.

'Alice … stop where you are … listen to me … I didn't mean to snarl at you there … sorry I called you … a bitch … we'll be all right … just you wait there.' For some reason this panted attempt at reconciliation frightened her more than any amount of shouting. With a heart that pounded like a drum in her chest and a lump in her throat, she began to move as fast as she could along the stony path. She did not run because that way would have led to certain death. She was well above the trees now. One false step would launch her on a wingless flight that could only end in one way – in death.

Alice made her way along the path. Her idea was simple

enough; to find a natural slope going away from where she was. The woods were getting much thicker now that she was away from the place where Shannon had made his ambush. If she could get into these she was certain that he would not see her. She had no idea what she was going to do after that but she was fairly certain she would be able to lose him.

Despite the blow to his head he was beginning to catch up with her.

The stony ground widened out to a rough platform quite high above the green canopy of the trees. If she could get beyond this, she saw the path swoop downwards to a place where she could get down and into the woods. Her heart soared at the thought. She leapt forward, knowing that in a scant few seconds she would be free of him.

She was brought up short as her hair was grabbed from behind. Who would have thought she would be betrayed by her long tresses? Her scalp felt as if it had been set on fire, so tightly did he hold her hair. He eased her round to face him so that he was standing, breathing in her face. His expression was not one of anger at all, but triumph. His face was red from exertion and there was a mark on the side of his face where she had hit him. His mouth was a little bloody, his white teeth marred by the redness as he mocked her.

'Alice, Alice, what's the matter? Come back to the cave, it's all over. We'll shelter for a few more days, and then we'll ride out of here with the cash and get married. I don't blame you for being frightened; it's a real strange place. Come on.'

As he spoke he relaxed his grip on her hair, but somehow

a knife appeared in his hand.

'As I say, come on, let's go.'

'I will never have anything else to do with you.' The hatred that filled her burst out. She forgot where she was and spat into his face, then punched him square between the eyes.

'You bitch, you're going to pay for that.' He lunged out blindly with his knife and she stepped backwards, jerking her head free from his remaining grip. Only her feet did not meet with solid ground. Screaming loudly, flailing her arms, Alice fell through the thick canopy of leaves and disappeared from sight. Her screams were abruptly cut off.

She was gone for good.

Panting, Shannon wiped the spittle off his face then looked over the edge. He did not know how high they were off the ground, but it was a good distance. He stood up and looked around. He could plainly see that there was a slope that would allow him to get down to her body, but he was filled with doubt. What if he went down and discovered the gunman wounded but still alive? It would take Blaze a moment to pick off a man descending from a higher point. He was aware of a vague regret. He had wanted Alice Lovell in his own way, if only she hadn't been so stubborn. The idea of marrying into the Lovell fortune hadn't been so bad, either. She had caused her own downfall, literally in this case.

Shannon pulled back from the edge of the path and began to walk towards the cave in a decisive manner. There was nothing left for him to do now but pack up the basic necessities and get out of here. Those who had been warned about the kidnapping of Alice would be looking for a man and a young woman; he could adopt another name and get away before the authorities caught up with him. Besides, he had the money; he brightened up at the thought and his pace quickened.

He was disturbed only by the thought of Blaze. What if the gunman had survived and was on his trail right now?

Well that would be an interesting battle. He might be the man who killed Blaze in a stand-up fight. It was a good thought.

Just the same, he hurried to get back and prepare for departure.

CHAPTER FOURTEEN

Blaze ran towards the source of the screams, which were abruptly cut off, and found that he was in an area where the undergrowth had deepened again and he could barely move. That was when he found the girl. That she had fallen from above was obvious, given the fact that she was caught in a thicket of elm branches just above his head. Despite the wound in his side he was still a fairly agile man; he climbed up by putting his feet on the gnarled trunk of the great elm and used the lower branches as levers. When he was level with where she lay, he swung out his legs, wrapped them around the tangle of branches, and pulled downwards. The branches might have supported the weight of the girl, but they were no match for a grown man as well. Her body slid forward and was deposited in the thick bushes that grew just above ground level.

He got back down from the tree. His body was shaking and he was soaked in perspiration. The wound at his side was still leaking, but at least he had achieved his aim of getting the girl away from the branches in which she had been caught. He went over to the girl and saw that she was covered in many minor cuts and scratches, but she had survived a fall from a height that would have killed most people. She was unconscious, whether from the impact or just from fright, he was unable to tell. This did not worry him too much. Instead what he did was pick up her limp body and make his way back to the stream that had helped reduce his swollen ankle. He laid her down on the solid dark loam beside the stream, and then splashed cold water on her face.

The girl moaned and gasped, then opened her eyes. What she saw above her was Blaze's swinging hair as he leaned over her, and a glimpse of the ruined side of his face. She must have thought that she was dead and that she was faced with a denizen of Hell.

The girl opened her mouth in a frightened O and was about to give the biggest scream of her life, when a calloused but not callous hand cut off her cries. As he put one hand over her mouth, Blaze put a finger from the other to his lips and nodded towards the trees.

'Watch out,' he said in a calm, quiet voice barely above a whisper. The implication was obvious; they knew who they had to watch out for.

'You're not going to scream if I take my hand away, are you?' His words were not just a question, but almost a statement of what she must not do. The girl gave a brief nod and he let her go.

Blaze stepped back to give her space to move. In his dark red shirt and black, slightly tattered coat that almost trailed to the ground, along with that bizarre face, he had the look of a creature from another world. For a second she even doubted once more that she was still alive at all. She sat up and groaned, her long legs splayed out in front of her, and then pushed up from the ground. Ever the female, she immediately touched her hair and face.

'I must look a terrible fright,' she said, realizing how odd this must sound to the creature she was facing. She bathed her face in the cool waters of the stream. The man watched her, standing with a calm stillness that said he was making sure she was not suffering too many ill-effects from her fall.

'Thank you, Blaze,' she said, feeling much better from her brief acquaintance with the stream.

'How do you know my name?'

'River knew who you were,' said the girl.

'And you're Alice,' he said, using her name to reassure her. 'Your father would like to see you again.'

Those words were enough to let her know that he was not just some random stranger, and that he knew about her and wanted to help. His voice was so low it was almost hypnotic and she found herself, despite her circumstances, gripped by a strange fascination for him. He did not so much betray his emotion by a word or a look but she had the impression that he wanted out of the glade. He was just making sure that she understood everything that she had to know before he left.

'Don't go,' she said. His face, the mobile half, expressed only regret.

'I'm sorry, I have to go now, and this might be my only chance to catch River Shannon.' He did not really believe this was the case, but he wanted to impress upon the girl the urgency of the situation. He looked around and gave a brief nod.

'This place is well sheltered. You should do all right here. Just rest up and leave everything to me.' He spoke with such reassurance that she immediately felt safe with him. After her fall he had carried her for quite a distance; even then, barely conscious, she had felt the power in him. He was not a man to overstate his case.

He got up and began to depart. He was not trying to force his way through the woods, but was taking the easiest route, which meant heading back down and along to where he had been ambushed and his fine horse killed. He would go carefully then, and intercept Shannon.

As he walked away the girl got up and began to follow him. He turned and put his hands on her shoulders. She could smell dried sweat on him and the tang of tobacco on his breath.

'Alice, your life was saved by some kind of a miracle. They don't come along in pairs. Please stay where you are.' He had a quiet, almost hypnotic tone. The girl sat down on one of the bigger rocks, and this time when he departed she did not attempt to follow, but instead immersed herself in the green stillness of the woods, with only the rustle of hidden wildlife to keep her company. Sitting there, she became aware of the sting of the many cuts to her face, arms and legs, and the dull aches where bruises would soon appear to blacken her skin.

She was not her father's daughter for nothing, there was a firm set to her jaw and a gleam in her eye that did not rest well with her present state of ease. Barely five minutes after the departure of her new hero, Alice jumped to her feet, groaning a little at the effort, and followed her defender.

Shannon was not about to fool himself that he was in the clear. For one thing, he had the money to deal with and that took a great deal of time. He repacked his loot into a large pair of saddle bags which he strapped onto his horse. It was an absorbing task. At first he thought of the girl as he was putting away the money.

What a fine creature she had been. He had loved her as much as he was capable of loving another human, which to say was not all that much. But she had fitted into his picture of what he, Shannon, had wanted from life. His needs were simple: plenty of money, a beautiful wife and his own land. What a pity she had turned out to be such an hysterical young fool. He had given her plenty of chances and she had destroyed them all, killing herself in the process. He made sure that he had packed everything he needed, including canteens full of water, and then checked that his horse's cinch straps had been properly tightened.

He was cautious about riding out, but it was still fairly early on in the day and if he had to, he would camp out all night in Whispering Canyon, the entrance to Hidden Valley. He was pretty certain that both the girl and the gunman were dead. He had not heard a thing from the woodlands since Blaze had moved into them. That would be a bonus when he got to meet some of his old criminal friends. He could boast that he had killed the famous Jubal Thorne.

Then his face tightened. There would be no more time

with criminals. He was going to make sure that from now on he would get his own land, his own men and build his own ranch. He would leave his past behind him.

That was when he heard the breaking of the twig, a noise that could have only been made by a human being.

Normally he would have stayed and looked for the source of the noise, but it had been very faint. He grinned to himself; if Thorne was still alive then he was on foot, and at least one of his feet was damaged. He would not be travelling far that way. With this thought in mind, Shannon got on his mount and spurred it onwards, out between some white oaks and onto the open plain. In a few short seconds he would be free and away from this place that had turned out to have a curse on it.

He could not resist the urge to look back. A dark figure emerged from the woodland many yards away and raised two Peacemakers. Shannon could not resist the urge to laugh out loud at this puny attempt to stop him. He was quite aware of how inaccurate handguns were at a distance. Someone would have to be an extraordinary marksman to bring him down.

He heard the twin explosions and his horse gave a convulsive heave and began to stumble. It had been hit on one of its forelegs. That was enough. The animal could no longer bear the weight of the man or the money bags and began to collapse to one side. Shannon threw his body off the animal and ran. Another fusillade of shots came at him. He zigzagged as he headed back for the woodlands, but he didn't have to get that far. Large rocks of volcanic origin stuck out of the plain here and there. He came to one of these and threw his body behind this makeshift shelter. Feverishly he reached for his handgun, the one that had coolly dispatched all those *vaqueros*.

This situation was a lot different. They had not been expecting an attack in their own territory and had been unarmed when he shot them, the best way, in his opinion, to carry out such a deed. Blaze was not only armed, he knew how to use his guns. Blaze came forward, limping a little at the effort but still relentlessly closing the distance between the two of them. Shannon ducked out from behind the rock to fire at the gunman and several bullets zinged past his head, so that he had to shelter again without firing a single bullet.

He raised his hand and fired a random shot in the direction of the hunter, but this had no effect since Blaze was no fool and varied his steps without slowing down. Shannon knew that he would soon have a deadly gunman looming over him. He rolled away from the rock, other gunshots whining past him as he did so. He drew a deep breath and stood up to face his opponent. They both had guns in their hands so it was an equal fight. It was just a question now of which one would get their deadly shot in first. From where Shannon stood it was going to be Blaze.

But what the hunter had forgotten in his onward quest was that he had already fought that day. In rescuing the girl and questing through the woodlands he had committed the mistake of his life. His anger had reached boiling point.

He had fired too many bullets.

Both his Colts gave empty clicks as he tried to fire upon his enemy. Shannon gave a twisted grin. He was going to be known after all as the man who defeated Blaze. He had one or two bullets left and he was a good shot. He would get him in the heart.

But just as he raised his pistol to fire, there was a noise from the line of trees nearby. A lithe female form came crashing out of the undergrowth, ran forward at speed and a short branch whirled through the air, catching Shannon on the side of the head. Blaze crouched down as this happened, dropped his guns and pulled a snub nosed revolver from a hidden armpit holster.

Shannon gave a furious roar and wiped his eyes free of the shards of bark that had showered down from the makeshift club, but it was too late. The revolver barked like an angry dog and Shannon took three bullets to his heart. Shannon's once handsome features twisted into ugly lines as he fell to his knees, then face forward on the ground. It took only a few seconds for him to die.

The girl ran forward, sobbing her heart out. She ignored Blaze, going to the side of her former lover instead, turning his body over and cradling his head while the tears ran down her face. This was the man who had been hers for however short a time before he showed his true colours. She was not really weeping for the man in her arms, but for the life that could have been if he had been telling the truth. Wisely, Thorne remained where he was until she let go of Shannon and stood up.

Thorne came over and put a hand on her shoulder.

'Come on, Alice, it's time to go home.'

CHAPTER FIFTEEN

A few days later, a scarred gunman rode into town accompanied by a young woman and another horse, one of the big chestnuts, on a leather string. Over the back of the spare horse was a bundle that had been wrapped well in a slick, oil-based material and then wrapped again in corn sacking so that the object little resembled the man it had once been. The horse also carried two packed saddle bags.

Blaze rode up to the big house on the hill with the girl. Her father came out of the building; Ella was in the background twisting her hands together. Alice dismounted and stood before her father.

'Girl or not, I should give you a whopping,' he growled. 'The sleepless nights you've caused Ella.'

The girl knew that her father was really talking about himself, a fact that the tough old miner could never admit. She embraced her father, who looked more frail than she had ever seen him, and then turned her attentions to Ella, who immediately scolded her for giving them all such a fright. Mikey appeared and rapidly climbed the hill to her home.

'You've been gone a bit,' said that young man, but was tactful enough not to press the point.

Alice was wordless, filled with anguish at the agony she had caused herself and others with her actions.

'Where's Clayton?' her father asked the gunman, who had remained on his horse and looked just about ready to leave.

'Got his final reckoning in a battle,' said the gunman.

'You must have quite a story to tell,' said the industrialist. 'Come in and I'll see to it that you're fed and watered and you can tell us all about it.'

'Thing is, you've got an extra guest here,' said Thorne blandly; his eyes strayed to the burden on the horse beside him.

'Lord, is that what I think it is?'

'I guess so.'

Alice did not need to be reminded. She looked up to Blaze.

'Thanks for all your help, Jubal Thorne.' But there was a tone in her voice that said she would be glad if they never met again. It was not hard for Blaze to understand why this was the case. He might have rescued her, and she might have helped in the downfall of Shannon, but ultimately Blaze had killed a man she had once loved. Every moment she was in his presence would remind her of her own great folly and memories that she wanted to put into her past.

'Clayton's mortal remains have been taken care of,' said Blaze. 'He died a hero, and that's all I'm saying for now.'

'Sure going to miss him as a friend as much as anything else,' the older man said. He did not elaborate on the subject but it was obvious that he took the loss hard. There was a look in his eyes that said he was going to be displeased with his daughter over the demise of the sheriff; the rider could sense this.

'Don't blame Alice for anything; she had nothing to do with what happened to Clayton. In fact, if we had just been looking for her he would have been back safe and sound.' He was pleased to see the look of relief on Lovell's face now that he knew the search for his daughter had nothing to do with the death of a fine sheriff.

Old man Lovell struck his cane forcibly on the ground.

'Thorne, can't you see what this means? Stay here, it's up to the voters, but if I make the proposal it's a certainty you'll get in. Stay here and become the sheriff, we need a man of your calibre.'

'You already have a man who's good enough for the job,' said Blaze, looking directly at Mikey who returned his gaze with a look of frank regard. 'This young man nearly stopped a thundering carriage on his own. It's not his fault that he didn't succeed. Clayton wanted to go because of your daughter; Mikey will stay because she's back. He's young, but that's a condition that will soon pass. Give him a chance.'

When she heard Thorne's words regarding Mikey, Alice looked at that young man as if seeing him for the first time, then burst into tears and ran into the house. Mikey started to go after her, then thought better of the matter and remained where he was.

'You're a wise man,' said Blaze. 'Leave her alone, she knows what she was missing, believe me, and promise when you two are together, you'll never raise the subject of River Shannon.'

'I guess I can do that,' said Mikey stolidly.

'Good.' Blaze began to turn his horses in preparation for leaving.

'Wait, what about your reward?' said Lovell.

'What reward?'

'For rescuing my daughter.'

'Give the two of 'em whatever it was as a wedding present,' said Blaze. He moved onwards as always.

After he had a day of rest in the very hotel in which he had encountered the Ferris brothers – his passenger wasn't going anywhere and it had been a hard three days in the wilderness – Blaze completed his trip to Harrisville and handed over the body and the money. Once the amount Shannon had used for his own purposes had been accounted for, he received his reward.

It was an amount many a man would have spent on booze and women, but he put some of it away and went to El Frontera.

Though few knew it, Dan Clayton had a good woman whom he had been looking after. That woman received enough money to keep her for years to come.

As for Blaze, his restless soul moved him on.

There was work to be done.